BAD BOY

BOOK TWO OF THE GOOD BOY, BAD BOY DUET

MEGAN LOWE

Cover Design: Pretty In Ink Creations

Photographer: 6:12 Photography by Eric McKinney

Model: Mark S

Editing: Hot Tree Editing

Formatting: Pretty In Ink Creations

E-Book ASIN: B096RJ93T5

Paperback: 978-0-6486536-2-2

❀ Created with Vellum

For those who want to be better;
For the misunderstood;
For those who are fighting battles we cannot see.
For anyone who has had to fight to be with the person they love.

JAMES

James (18):

Not interested in any bullshit drama, just want a good time, not a long time.

Nothing serious.

No feelings, no hurt.

CHAPTER 1

Kevin drops his hands, and I put the pedal to the floor. Next to me, Connor does the same. I didn't want this, but when I saw him and Thomas in the closet? I gave him a rose; I said the word. I want him. I want to be with him. But obviously I'm too late. I'm always being forgotten. Or overlooked or ignored. What's the difference here?

My parents don't care about me, and now Connor doesn't either. I thought he did. Obviously I was wrong. I just... didn't think I was this time.

I look over, and Connor is neck and neck with me, not giving an inch. I didn't think he would.

We shouldn't be doing this. I'm putting him in danger. I hated the idea of him racing, and now it's me he's up against? I'm fucked-up.

Connor was, no, Connor *is* a beacon of light for me. I loved our conversations when I was just James, and not only the ones that ended with us coming all over ourselves. With him, I could be free. I could pretend I don't have to hide who I am from my parents. I could pretend that maybe one day, in an alternate universe, I could have someone like him in my life.

The finish line is fast approaching, but I can't stop, won't stop until I can outrun all the shit that's plaguing me. It's not even about me and Connor anymore. Maybe it never was. Now, it's about me and my problems and the open road in front of me.

We hit the finish line, and I have no idea who's first. I don't care.

Instead, I put my foot down further, my Chevelle responding with a purr.

Another quick look shows Connor with me, shouting something. I can probably guess what he's saying, and even though he's confused, he sticks with me.

He goes with me, side by side, before pulling behind me when the road dictates it.

I wish I could run away. Disappear and never be seen or heard of again.

Once again, Connor pulls up alongside me, his arms outstretched. I look at him, at his handsome face, the blondish hair I want to run my fingers through, the blue eyes I want to spend hours staring into. God, do I want him.

I'm so lost in him, and he's probably wondering what the fuck is going on. Neither of us sees the other car until it's too late.

Connor swerves, his car eventually tipping and rolling. I watch in my rearview as he flips once, twice, three times, four.

I pull on my handbrake, drifting the car around.

Connor's car has come to a stop upside down.

"Connor!" I scream, running up to the wreck. "Connor!"

I tear his airbags to the side, finding him upside down, still belted into his seat.

"Connor!" I scream again.

There's a large gash on his head, blood running everywhere. His eyes are struggling to stay open, and his breathing is labored, so labored.

The smell of gas is thick in the air, and I know it's only a matter of time before the car goes up.

I race back to my car to get my knife so I can cut his seat belt and get him out. I also grab my phone and call 911 as I run back to him.

"Babe, I'm gonna cut you free, okay?" I say to him, even though his eyes aren't open.

I cut him loose and drag him away from the wreck, sirens filling the air.

"Babe," I say, cradling his head in my lap.

No response.

"I'm so sorry," I tell him. "This is all my fault. I never should've organized this, never should've kept going. But why did you follow me? You're so stupid, Connor. You should've let me go. You should've let me go the moment you found out who I am. If I was smarter, I never should've matched with you. The minute I saw your smile on your profile I knew I was in trouble, but I couldn't help myself. I wanted you. I *still* want you." I press a kiss to his lips. "Please be okay."

The paramedics arrive and run to us.

"His car flipped," I tell them. "It flipped over and over and over and over. I saw it. I saw him. I got him out. I could smell gas and I knew the car, it could go up at any moment."

The paramedic nods at me. "You got him out, that's good. But we need you to let him go so we can examine his injuries."

"You'll look after him?" I ask.

He nods again. "We'll do our very best, I promise."

I move out from underneath him. "His name is Connor. He has an older sister and a younger brother. Their parents both died from cancer. He's from Michigan and loves the Lions but he agreed to be a Cubs fan because of Kris Bryant."

The paramedic pats me on the shoulder. "Thanks. You did good, man."

"Yeah?"

"Yeah. See? Look." He hitches his head toward the wreck of Connor's car, where the fire department is putting out the fire that started. When did it start? I didn't see, didn't realize. All I saw was Connor. All I *see* is Connor.

"Oh."

"Are you hurt?"

I shake my head. "Just Connor."

"He's got a tension pneumothorax," one of the other paramedics says. "We gotta get him out of here."

"Can I go with him?" I ask.

"If I say no, will you drive yourself?"

I nod. "I have to be with him."

"All right," he says. "You're in shock, so there's no way I want you driving right now, but you have to let us do our job, okay?"

I nod.

"Good, let's go."

CHAPTER 2

My eyes are glued to the monitor connected to Connor's chest, his heartbeat fast but steady. The paramedics managed to reinflate his lung, but he's still going to need surgery.

"You going to get that?" the one who let me ride with them says.

"Huh?" My eyes never leave the monitor.

"Your phone. It's been ringing nonstop."

I fish it out of my pocket and only briefly take my eyes off Connor's heart's squiggly line to see it's Jase calling.

"Hey," I say when I answer.

"Hey?" he asks. "Fucking hey? What the hell happened, Cav? You guys just kept driving, and no one knows what happened or where you are and Connor's not answering his phone." He's yelling loud enough for even the driver to hear us. Not that I blame him.

"I'm sorry, it's all my fault. I just kept driving, I didn't think he'd follow me."

"That's all great and everything, but where the fuck are

you guys? And why isn't my brother answering his fucking phone?"

"There was an accident."

"An accident? What kind of accident? Is everyone okay? Where's Connor? Is he all right?"

"He—" I try to swallow my sob. "He…. His car…. Ambulance…."

"What? Cav, you're not making any sense. Is my brother okay?"

A hand appears, breaking my visual of Connor's monitor.

"Give the phone to me," the paramedic says.

I hand it to him, Jase yelling at me clear for anyone to hear.

"Hey, who is this?" he asks. "Hi, Jase. My name is Toby and I'm a paramedic with the Chicago Fire Department. Connor is your brother, is that correct?"

I nod, even though he's not asking me.

"As your friend told you, there was an accident. Connor's car flipped, and he's hurt. Before you panic," Toby says, talking over Jase, "he's stable for now, but he does have a punctured lung, a pretty bad concussion, and some really nasty cuts. We're taking him to Chicago General. Can someone take you there?"

I take my eyes off the monitor to gesture to Toby to give me the phone.

Jase is saying something about an Uber when I get the phone to my ear.

"Jase, where's Thomas?" I ask. Even though I hate to think about my former BFF and Connor's so-called "boyfriend," he promised he'd watch over Jase. Even though their relationship is a sham, I still thought he could at least do one thing.

"I don't know," he sobs. "He just fucking left, everyone fucking left, and I have no idea where I am or how to get anywhere and Connor was in an accident and Amy is going to flip."

"It'll be okay," I promise. "Order an Uber and get to the hospital. I'll be there waiting."

"Is Connor going to be okay?" he asks in a small voice.

"Connor's strong, he's a fighter. He's going to be just fine."

"Okay." He's silent for a moment. "Cav? You're looking after him, right? You won't let anything bad happen?"

"I promise I'll do my best to make sure he's fine."

"Okay, good."

"Hurry up and order that Uber, and I'll meet you at the hospital, okay? Chicago General."

"Yup, I got it. I'll, um, see you soon."

"Cav...."

"I'll take care of him, I promise. You know I'd never let anything bad happen to him." Ignoring, of course, the fact that Connor is in this mess because of me in the first place.

"Yeah, I know. I'll, um, see you soon." He ends the call.

"You care for him a lot," Toby says.

"Who? Jase?"

"Yeah, him, but I was meaning your boyfriend, Connor."

I give a wry chuckle. "He's not my boyfriend. He's sorta dating my best friend." Who couldn't even keep up the charade enough to figure out what happened to his boyfriend. I mean, I know Thomas doesn't care about Connor, but to show it outright? If I didn't already know Thomas is a bastard, I know it now.

"Oh, um, okay then. But it would still be useless to ask you out, right?"

"Shouldn't you be focused on your patient?" I grit out, the steady rhythm of Connor's heartbeat giving me some comfort.

I hear rather than see him shrug, his shirt rubbing against the back of his seat as he moves. "He's stable for the moment, and we're only a couple of minutes out from the hospital."

"And that kind of attitude is okay with the CFD?"

Another shrug. "A guy's gotta take a shot whenever it's presented to him."

I shake my head.

"And it's not like you're all that better. Here you are with you *best friend's* boyfriend. He's not even yours."

"He should be," I say before I realize what I've said.

"But he's not."

"Just like I won't be yours. How about you stop worrying about me and my love life and do your fucking job and make sure he's okay."

I take my eyes off the monitor for a second to see him hold up his hands. "Sorry."

The ambulance shudders to a stop, and a moment later, the doors open.

Toby spurts Connor's stats and an update on his condition as a team of doctors and nurses pull him out of the ambulance.

I follow behind, not wanting to let him out of my sight.

"I'm sorry," a nurse says, stopping me when we get to a door marked Authorized Personnel Only. "You can't come back here."

"But I need to be with him," I tell her.

"I'm sorry, you can't. We need to do an assessment, and you'll be in the way." She doesn't say that if something goes wrong, I don't want to see that and they don't want to have to deal with my emotional ass if and when that happens.

"I promised his brother I'd keep him safe."

"How about you transfer that to me?" she asks.

"C-Can I see him? Just to tell him what's happening? To s-say g-g-g—" I can't say goodbye. I swallow. "To tell him I'll see him soon?"

She smiles. "Quickly, but please try not to get in our way."

I nod, and she leads me back. There's a flurry of activity around Connor's bed.

"He's going to be okay, right?" I ask the nurse.

"We're doing our best."

It's not a yes. But it's also not a no. I guess all I can do is hope and pray. I've never prayed before, not really sure how to do it, but for him, I'd be willing. The senator would drop dead if she heard me say that, but her brand of Christianity isn't exactly kind to people like me. Still, I'd be willing to do anything if it meant he'd be okay, for me to have a second chance with him.

The nurse directs me near Connor's head. "Quickly."

I bend down and press my lips to his forehead. "I'm so sorry, baby. I never should've suggested this, but I was so mad and it was stupid, *so* stupid. Please be okay. I don't know what I'll do without you. If you come back to me, I promise I'll do whatever you need me to do. I-I... I love you, Connor." A tear drops on his cheek. Gently, I wipe it away.

"We'll look after him," the nurse who brought me in says.

I nod.

"If you wait outside, I'll give you updates when I can, okay?"

I nod again. "Yeah. Thanks. For everything, letting me in here and everything."

She smiles and squeezes my hand. "You're welcome, honey. Now, he has to have some tests and then he'll go into surgery."

"Let's go," one of the doctors says.

"He'll be okay, I promise," she calls as they whisk Connor away.

CHAPTER 3

About twenty minutes after I went back to the waiting room, Jase rushes in, hair a mess, eyes wild. Literally thirty seconds later, an older female version of him runs in.

"Jase!" she yells. "Where is he? What the hell happened?"

"I don't know." He looks around, spots me, and comes over.

"Cav—"

"He's okay," I tell him—them—before they can ask again. "He has a likely concussion, some cuts, bruises, and bumps. He also—" I swallow. "—has a punctured lung. They're taking him into surgery."

"Can we see him?" Amy asks.

I shake my head. "He's having some tests done first, and from there, surgery. One of his nurses has promised to give me updates though."

"And you are?" she asks.

"Cavanaugh McLaughlin, ma'am. A, um, friend of Jase and Connor's."

"Cav, what happened?" Jase asks.

I shake my head. "It was stupid and all my fault. I kept driving, and he kept trying to get me to pull over. I should've listened, should've stopped. We, um, didn't see the other car until it was too late. He swerved but ended up rolling." I look to Amy. "Please know it was one hundred percent my fault. Connor was only trying to do right and stop me."

"You were racing?"

I nod. "Yes, ma'am."

She turns to Jase. "Why didn't you tell me?"

Jase looks down at his feet.

"With all due respect, ma'am, what was he supposed to say?" I ask.

"He was supposed to tell me his brother is being an ass and likely to get himself killed, which he damn near has done whether or not you take responsibility. And stop calling me ma'am! I'm twenty-three, for fuck's sake." With that she storms off to the information desk, presumably to get, well, information.

"Have you heard from Thomas?" I ask Jase as we sit down.

He shakes his head. "But I don't think he has my number."

I pull my own phone out. No notifications pop up, especially none from Thomas.

"What happened with him?"

Jase shrugs. "As soon as Kevin started the race, he just walked away. I think...."

"You think what?"

He sighs. "I think he went and picked up one of the girls who was hanging around."

I nod. "Of course he did."

"But I don't *know* that," he covers quickly. "After you guys disappeared, I kind of lost him in the crowd and confusion."

I shake my head. "He doesn't need you to cover for him," I tell him.

"He's Connor's boyfriend."

I raise an eyebrow. "Is he? I mean, really?"

He slumps in his chair. "I don't know what Connor sees in him."

"He saw a way to get back at me. They both did." When Thomas first went after Connor, I wasn't sure what his endgame was. I sure as fuck know it now.

"It won't last. Connor doesn't even like him."

"So why's he still with him?" I ask. But I know that answer. Connor's still with Thomas because I was too much of a pussy to admit I wanted to be with him, to take the steps I need to, to be with him. But I did. I said the words. I'll do it. I'll take the steps. Whatever I need to do to be with Connor, I'll do.

"I don't know, but I *know* he likes you, that he wants to be with you."

I nod. "I want to be with him, too," I whisper. "When Connor's better, I'm going to fix things, make them right. We're supposed to be together, destined to, even. I can't fight what I feel for him. I've tried, and it didn't work." I look over at Jase, the same eyes, similar features as his brother. "I'm in love with Connor."

He smiles. "Finally. Took you long enough to admit it."

I shrug. "It won't be easy, and I know I have a lot to make up for, but I will do it. I promise."

CHAPTER 4

When I told Jase me being with Connor wouldn't be easy, I didn't mean just between Connor and me.

The honorable Carla McLaughlin, Senator for Illinois, is a darling for the Conservative Party. Having a son in a same-sex relationship would not be a good look.

So, I've been the good son. I've been discreet. I've gone to events with girls on my arm, only to get rid of them as soon as I could. I've been good. Until Connor.

He makes me want to say "fuck it" to everything and everyone, and right now, if the senator were here, I probably would.

I love Connor. I'm in love with him. I think I fell for him during our first conversation. I tried, *really* tried not to fall for him, but that body? That mind? That spirit he has? Who could resist?

The senator, that's who. My whole life, all I've ever heard is how fags are unnatural and against the will of God, as if we had a choice in whom we love.

And my dad won't be any help. He's as subservient as they come. The senator has well and truly got him under her thumb. He won't even breathe in her direction, let alone disagree with her. To be honest, he kind of makes me sick. I've never seen anyone bow to her as my father does. But then, I do the same, don't I? Nobody fucks with Carla McLaughlin, especially her family.

I've tried to be discreet. I'm *always* discreet. I even gave Connor the same spiel when we first started talking, but as soon as I saw him in Windswept's parking lot that first day, I knew it wouldn't work. I knew I was in trouble.

He's everything I want wrapped up in one neat package. I tried fighting it. I did everything in my power to turn him against me, to get him to forget me, to move on.

And then Thomas happened.

I laughed, so sure Connor wouldn't fall for Thomas's shit, that he'd keep him at arm's length. Never in my wildest dreams did I ever think they'd date.

Thomas and I have always had a strained relationship. Sure, he's my best friend, or *was*, but I always felt like there was something about me he didn't like. I know he didn't understand why I went after Connor when he first got to Windswept, but I thought he'd go along with it, just like he's gone along with everything else.

But he didn't.

Somehow he saw through my pretense and identified my weakness. I don't know how he knows about my feelings for Connor, or if it's just a hunch, but it's clear he knows something, and he's using that to his advantage. He took his shot, and I can't blame him for that. I hate him for it. But I can't blame him. If it were my enemy, I would too.

But he wasn't supposed to fall in love with Connor. Connor was mine. *Is* mine.

But why isn't Thomas here?

Jase said he saw him picking up some chick during the race. Why would he do that?

I shake my head. I can't worry about that, I can't worry about *any* of it. The only thing that matters, the only thing that will *ever* matter, is Connor.

CHAPTER 5

"He's in surgery," Amy says when she comes back over.

"Is he okay?" I ask as Jase opens his mouth.

She shoots me a look before answering. "His scans came back okay. He has a concussion but no bleeding on the brain. His lung was punctured, and he ruptured his spleen, but they're taking care of that now."

"He ruptured his spleen?" I ask, collapsing back in the uncomfortable plastic chair.

"Yes, he did." She turns to me. "So, do you want to tell me exactly how this all happened? And don't bullshit me either and tell me it was all you. I know my brother; he's not one to just go along with things for funsies."

I nod. "Yes, ma'am."

She huffs and I hold up a hand in apology.

"The race itself Connor agreed to," I tell her. "I could tell he didn't really want to race, well race *me*, at least not because of the reason we were both pretending was the motivation."

She cocks her head to the side but doesn't say anything.

"The race was fine. It was straightforward, but at the finish line I didn't want to stop. I was angry, I was frustrated so I just... kept going."

"Did you lose?" Amy asks. "Is that why you were angry?"

"I don't know who won," I say.

"We couldn't tell either," Jase adds. "Kevin wanted a rematch, but then you guys kept going."

I nod.

"So if you weren't angry about losing, why were you angry?" Amy asks.

I blow out a breath. "A whole heap of things. My parents, my friends, shit at school... Take your pick."

"And you kept going," she prompts.

I nod. "Connor followed me, tried to get me to stop. He, um, didn't want me to go off the deep end, I guess."

"And now it's him who's hurt."

I look up, straight into her eyes, so much like her brother's. "Believe me, if I could swap places with him, I would in a heartbeat," I tell her as my phone rings. The number on the screen belongs to the senator's chief of staff. I decline the call.

"That may be so, Mr....." She trails off.

"McLaughlin. Cavanaugh McLaughlin."

"As in Senator Carla McLaughlin's son?"

I nod.

She chuckles. "Of course Connor would involve a senator's son in his mess." She shakes her head.

"To be fair, he didn't know I'm the senator's son when we first met, and the race was my idea, not his."

She waves her hand at me. "It doesn't matter. This whole thing is typical of Connor. I thought…." She shakes her head again. "It's late. You should probably get home."

My heart lurches at the thought of leaving. I clear my throat. "Ah, if it's okay with you, I'd like to stay. You know, so I know Connor's okay."

"Suit yourself," she says, reaching for her phone. "But for crying out loud, answer your phone, would you?"

Aiden, the senator's chief of staff, is still calling.

With a sigh, I answer.

"Please tell me the reports I'm getting of the senator's son partaking in an illegal street race and almost getting the other driver killed are some kind of liberal joke designed to put me in an early grave and take my focus away from the most important bill of the senator's career," he says before I can even say "hello."

"Is there such a thing as a *legal* street race?" I ask.

"What?" Aiden spits.

"You said 'partaking in an illegal street race' which, to my mind, makes me think there must be a legal one. If so, let me know where, and I'll be there with bells on."

"Are you kidding me right now?"

"I'm just thinking about how life would be so much easier for you if I was racing legally."

"You are—"

"One hell of a fuckup, yes, I know," I finish for him.

"Did you almost kill this guy?"

"Directly? No. Indirectly? Yes."

He blows out a breath. "This is a nightmare."

"Could be worse," I say. "I could be gay."

"Don't even joke about that!" he almost yells. "Do you know what that would do to our platform? Our image? Everything we've spent the past seventeen years building?"

"Why don't you fill me in?" I ask. "I've only heard it my entire life."

"I swear to all that is holy…. Why, Lord, did you have to bless me with the perfect candidate, only to curse her with the devil incarnate as her son?"

"I'm sure the senator asks the same question."

"Is the family going to sue?" he asks.

I pull the phone away from my face. "Um," I say to Amy. "I know this is a fucked-up question, but the senator's chief of staff would like to know if you have plans to sue me and, by extension, my parents?"

Amy looks up. "Why would I sue *you* for something my idiot brother did?"

"Because…. You know what, don't worry about it." I lift the phone. "His sister says no," I tell Aiden.

"You're still *there*?" he asks.

"Where else would I be?"

"Oh, I don't know. How about anywhere else but the scene of the crime, thus making you look guilty as sin?"

"Or maybe I look compassionate, apologetic, maybe even regretful."

"Hmm," he says. "Possibly. I mean, we could absolutely spin it that way."

"You do what you need to do, Aiden."

"Don't worry, I'll more than take care of the senator."

"Thank God," I say. "For a moment there I was actually worried."

"You little—"

"Delight, I know," I finish for him. "Take it easy," I say before I end the call.

"He really thought we'd sue?" Jase asks.

"Stranger things have happened."

"How is that your life?"

I shrug. "After a while you get used to it and it becomes normal."

"Nothing about what I heard of that conversation is normal."

"Just a day in the life of Senator Carla McLaughlin's inner circle."

"Is that why…?"

I shrug again, but nod.

"He wouldn't care, you know."

I nod again. "I know, but how is it fair to him?"

"How is it fair to *you*?"

CHAPTER 6

Seven hours after they took Connor for surgery, we're told he's moved to recovery.

"Can we see him?" I ask the same nurse who promised me she'd take care of him.

She smiles at me. "He's still coming out from the anesthesia, so he's groggy, but yes, you can see him."

"You don't mind, do you?" I ask Amy.

She waves me off. "It's fine. You go."

I turn back to the nurse, who says, "This way." Jase and I dutifully follow her down the hall and up to recovery.

"Is he okay?" I ask.

She nods. "We had to remove his spleen, which isn't a big deal, you can live just fine without one, and repair his lung, but he'll be okay. He also has a concussion and a few bumps and bruises, so he won't be up for much for a little while, but there's no reason he won't make a full recovery."

I blow out a breath. "Okay, good."

She stops outside a door. "Here we are."

My feet become leaden, my throat thick. "Ah… you go ahead," I manage to choke out to Jase.

"You sure?"

I nod.

He gives me a look, but goes in anyway.

"I wasn't lying when I said he's going to be okay," the nurse says.

"No, I know. I believe you too, it's just…."

"It can be a lot when a partner is seriously injured. He's young, so he should bounce back quickly, or at least quicker than someone three or four times his age, but it will still take time. He'll need you for that."

"That's the thing though," I say, running my hand through my hair. "He won't need me, won't *want* me. We're not…."

"Oh. I thought, given what you said to him in the ER, that you were."

I shake my head. "He's actually dating my best friend."

"Oh."

I chuckle. "Yeah. He thinks I kind of hate him. That's why we were racing, because I was mad at him."

"Well, um, I'm sure if he knew what devotion you showed him, he'd appreciate it."

"Yeah, maybe."

"Your best friend though…."

"Yeah, well, that's what he gets for taking my guy." I turn to the nurse. "Thank you for taking care of him and letting me see him."

She squeezes my forearm. "You're welcome, sweetie. And a tip? You don't find love like that," she tips her head toward Connor's room, "every day. You want him? Go get him. Fuck your best friend."

I choke out a laugh. "I'm not sure that's the advice people would usually give."

She shrugs. "Is your best friend the right guy for him?"

"Fuck no," I say.

"Are you?"

"I want to be. I want to try to be."

"Why try to be? Why not just be?"

"It's complicated." It's weird to be talking to someone who isn't Connor or Jase about this. But I can't deny that it feels… good to do so. Am I worried that people have seen me and will talk? Sure. But rumors are rumors, especially in politics. There's always someone making stuff up to put you off your game, or to weaken your position. The senator and Aiden have made it a rule to never believe anything until it's been confirmed. Listen to everything, but believe nothing. But there's a bit going on at moment, which buys me a little leeway. I hope.

"Until you can uncomplicate it, your best friend is always going to have the inside line."

"He's not even here!" I shout. "He didn't watch the race! He went and picked up some chick before our taillights disappeared. He doesn't care about him! I've been here, with him, every step of the way."

"Except this one," she points out.

I look at her. "He's going to hate me. Even more than he already does."

"Well, you did dare him to race you, a dare that ended up with him here, minus a spleen and with a hole in his lung."

"I thought you were supposed to make people feel better?"

"Patients," she clarifies. "You're not a patient. You're not even a significant other of a patient."

I clutch at my chest. "Damn, that hurt."

She shrugs. "But the good news is, you can change that."

"How do you know? You haven't even spoken to Connor; he's been unconscious."

"What if I were to tell you he woke up when we took him for scans and you were the person he was asking for?"

My heart leaps. "He did?"

"Well, no. He did wake up, but it was a whole lot of moaning and disorientation."

I shake my head. "You're really something. What's your name, by the way?" I realize that after everything, she's just Connor's nurse.

"Shelly."

I hold out my hand. "Cavanaugh. My friends call me Cav though."

She takes it. "It's nice to meet you, Cav."

"Who said you're my friend?" I ask, a smile on my face. It feels weird to do that; laugh and smile, while Connor's only a few feet away, hurt.

It's her turn to clutch her chest. "Now who's being mean?"

"Payback's a bitch, huh?"

She nods. "It is. So is life, but do me a favor?"

"What?"

"Don't let that one slip through your fingers. There's

something there; I *know* there is."

I nod, and she smiles.

"Good."

Jase walks out of Connor's room.

"How is he?" I ask.

He shrugs. "Okay. He's in a bit of pain, and he's hella drowsy, but he's okay."

"Good," I say as my shoulders drop. The tension that's been with me since I first pulled Connor out of the car, leaving me.

"He asked for you, you know," Jase adds.

My head swings to him so fast, it's a wonder I don't break my neck. "What?"

"He said he remembers the race, remembers chasing after you, trying to stop you. He remembers your voice, you know, after."

"Oh."

Jase nods. "He wants to see you."

I shift from foot to foot. "Oh, um, I don't, um, think I can do that."

"Why the hell not?" Shelly asks. "What did we just get done talking about?"

"I know, but—"

"No buts. The boy is asking for you. He's lying in a hospital bed after having surgery to remove an organ and to repair damage to another. Are you really going to stand here and say you can't?"

I glare at her, and she glares back.

"You're bossy as fuck, you know that?" I ask.

She shrugs. "Does it look like I care?"

I give her the finger.

"Stop stalling and get your ass in there."

My feet move in spite of my reluctance. It's all for naught anyway. When I get in there, Connor's asleep, his mouth open slightly, snoring quietly.

I pull the chair near his bed right up to it.

"I'm so fucking sorry, baby," I say, taking his hand and kissing the back of it. "I'm sorry for that stupid fucking race and what happened after. I'm sorry for what went on at school; I'm sorry for letting you go after Chloe's party; I'm sorry for everything with Thomas; I'm sorry I can't be with you, but fuck, baby, I want to try. Can we? I mean, I know you're with Thomas, but we both know why you're with him and he's not the one you should be with. Shelly, the nurse who's been with you since you came in, she thinks we make a great couple. I know we have a lot of stuff to figure out, but we can, can't we? Just be patient with me, okay? I'll get there, I swear I will, it just might take some time and it might get rocky, but it'll be okay." I kiss the back of his hand again. "I told you before that I love you, and it's true, I do. I love you so much, Connor. Just stick with me, and I promise it'll be all right."

Whether it was purely a reflex, or he did actually hear me, he squeezes my hand.

"Just us, baby, just us."

CHAPTER 7

I sat with Connor until he started to stir and I tagged Jase back in.

Shelly dropped by at the end of her shift, took one look at me sitting in the hallway, and rolled her eyes.

"I have been in," I tell her.

"And why aren't you in there now?"

"I'm giving him time with his brother?"

She shakes her head. "You're a mess."

I lean back in the plastic chair, resting my head on the wall behind me. "I know."

"But you will get your act together, right?"

I nod, my eyes closed. "I will." And I will. I know I have to talk to my parents, tell them my truth. It'll be hard, but I want to be with Connor and this is what I need to do so I can.

She pats me on the shoulder. "How about going home to get some rest, some food, and maybe a shower?"

"Hmm, yeah, maybe later."

"Cav…."

I open my eyes, scrubbing my hands over them, and sit up. "I'm good, I promise."

"You know you're no good to him if you run yourself into the ground."

"I know. I just don't want to leave him."

"Don't want to be with him, don't want to be without him. I know how that goes." She yawns.

"Looks like I'm not the only one who's beat," I say.

"The difference is, I'm going home," she retorts, getting up. "When I see you tonight, you better be in different clothes, mister."

I wave her off. "Yeah, yeah."

T he next thing I know, Jase is sitting down beside me.

"Shit, did I fall asleep?" I ask.

"That's not a bad thing," he replies.

"How is he?"

"Sore. He has a bit of a headache, and feels nauseous because of the concussion, but other than that, he's okay."

I nod. "Good."

"He was asking about you again."

My heart clenches. "D-Did you tell him I'm here."

"No."

I let out a breath.

"I didn't need to. He said he remembers hearing your voice, he's just not sure if it was a dream or not."

"Okay, that's okay."

"Is it?"

I nod. "Yeah, it is."

He shakes his head. "You're crazy."

"I just… don't want to, you know, upset him."

"But you're happy to sit out here like a creeper, slipping into his room to see him when he's asleep?"

"It's better this way."

"For you."

"For him too."

"What if he *wants* you in there? *While* he's awake?"

"That's…. It's…. He's—"

"More than capable of making his own decisions," he finishes for me.

"*Does* he want to see me?" I ask.

"I think he'd like the option of deciding for himself. I don't get it," Jase says. "It's clear you two like each other. I saw it when you were talking to him as James, and I see it now. Why the hell are you guys not together? Forget all that bullshit about your parents too."

"But I can't," I tell him. "As much as I'd love to do that, I can't. If, *when* I tell them, it's basically going to be the end of my life as I know it, not to mention the attention it's going to bring both me and Connor. If I can spare him that, I will."

"Even though it makes you miserable."

I shrug.

"And Thomas?" he asks.

"What about him?"

"He's not with Connor for the right reasons."

"And just what reasons are they?" the man himself asks as he walks down the hall with all the swagger of someone who's not at all concerned for his boyfriend's well-being.

"How about genuinely caring for him? Someone who did would've been here before now," Jase grits out, hands clenched.

Thomas laughs. "I had things to do. I couldn't get here until now."

"You were *at* the race," Jase points out. "If you'd been watching instead of trying to get in that girl's pants, you would've seen something happened and could've asked me when I called Cav."

"Where were you?" I ask quietly.

"I told you, I was busy."

"Is Jase right? Were you with some chick while your boyfriend was bleeding internally?"

"Looks like you had *my* boyfriend more than covered."

I charge at him, pushing him up against the wall. "You're a piece of shit."

"And you're in love with my boyfriend." He takes advantage of my surprise to knock my hands away. "What? You didn't think I knew you're gay? I didn't realize you were trying to hide it. I've known for a while, but I got my confirmation when Connor arrived at Windswept. And now, of course. Why do you think I went after him in the first place? For years, *years*, I've watched the whole world kneel at your feet. The Great Cavanaugh McLaughlin, the one who can never do anything wrong. But I knew. I saw behind the curtain. I know deep down you're not as great as you seem, how you're nothing but a pretender. You've pulled the wool over so many people's eyes but not me. You're just a pathetic little boy who's scared of his mommy and wants his daddy's love." He laughs and spreads his arms. "What's so great about that? Huh?"

"I...."

"You're what? Sorry? Not gay? 'Cause I don't believe either."

"W-What are you going to do?" I ask.

"About you?"

I nod.

He shrugs. "Dunno. Haven't decided yet. I quite like having the great Cavanaugh McLaughlin at my mercy. So I guess it depends."

"On what?"

"On how far you're willing to go in order to keep your secrets."

"You're blackmailing me?" I ask.

He picks at his nails. "Blackmail is such a dirty word when it's going to do me such good bringing you down. But yes, I suppose you could say I'm blackmailing you."

"What do you want?"

"I want you to suffer like I have all these years in your shadow. I want you to know what it's like living at someone else's mercy."

"And Connor?"

He waves a hand. "Connor is a way to help me make that happen."

"You son of a bitch." I slam him up against the wall.

He laughs. "Oh, come on, like you wouldn't have done that. You're the guy who pretends he killed someone so his reputation would skyrocket."

"I haven't pretended to do anything," I grit out. Max's

death… I may not be directly responsible, but in all the ways that matter, I am.

He laughs again. "Whatever you say, Cav. This is your world, I'm just playing in it."

"And your relationship with Connor is nothing more than a game."

He shrugs. "I mean, the guy is great and all, but he's not really my type, if you get what I mean."

"So you're not in love with him?"

"No, I'm not, but you are, and that's enough for me."

"What did I ever do to you?" I ask. "We've been best friends since we were born."

He shrugs. "I don't know. It's senior year, and I realized, 'what have I been doing all this time?' For eighteen years I've been your lackey, and I don't want to be. *Never* wanted to be."

"You've never been my lackey," I rebut.

"Lackey, slave, errand boy, same difference."

"I never forced you to do anything."

"But you did. You're Cavanaugh McLaughlin. Your word is gospel and the rest of us your apostles."

"I never—"

"Oh no, of course you didn't, but what choice did we have, huh?"

I stay silent.

He picks his nails some more. "So I decided to do something about it. I mean, really this is your own fault. You went after Connor *so* hard, I couldn't help but wonder why? I mean, why him? He was new, he hadn't done anything, but you took an *immediate* dislike to him.

The opportunity was too good to be true. Everything I've done has been because *you* started it."

"So you're punishing me."

"You're punishing yourself. I'm just digging the knife in deeper. The good news is, you can stop it. Just say the word, and I'll drop Connor. I'll drop everything."

"What? It's that simple?"

"I mean, sure. You come out in front of everyone—in some grand way; I think that would be fun—and you can have him."

My throat constricts. In some grand way? Knowing Thomas, that's going to involve a very public spectacle, and I can't. Yes, I want Connor, more than life itself, but look at the time it took me to get here. I shake my head. "I'm not ready," I tell him.

He laughs. "So don't come out. But know that *I* know your secret and I'm more than willing to use it. Or will I? Who knows? But I'm not going to deny it would be better for me if you *don't* do as I say. That way, I get to laud the fact that I know your secret over you. You'll always be wondering if or when I'll do something. How fun is that going to be?" He rubs his hands.

"You're insane."

"I learn from the best."

I shake my head. I know I said I'll do whatever it takes to be with Connor, but not like this, not with Thomas's threat acting like a knife to my throat.

"Are you fucking serious?" Jase asks. "This is for Connor."

"I'm sorry. I want him, I do, you know I do, but not like this."

"Then how?"

"Face it, little Siddell, your new bestie here, who used to be *my* bestie, is a pussy. He's scared. All his life he's had someone else to fight his battles and now, when push comes to shove, he can't do it."

"Jase," I say, hoping he can read the apology in my eyes.

"I thought you care about him? I thought you want him, love him."

"I did. I d-do."

"But you're happy to let him stay with Thomas?"

"Of course I'm not. But what he's asking…."

"I can't believe you."

"I will do it. I will. I just need time."

Jase shakes his head. "I think you should leave."

When I don't move, he gets up. "You need to go, Cav. Now."

"Jase—"

"Leave!" he yells, face red.

"Okay." I nod, Thomas's laugh echoing in my ears as I walk away.

CHAPTER 8

The McLaughlin estate was built on the shores of Lake Michigan in the 1800s and is as impressive and imposing as you'd assume it would be. It's uptight and pretentious, but it's home. Sort of.

"What the *hell* took you so long?" Aiden demands as he pounds down the stairs.

I ignore the question and brush past him, heading to the kitchen. After I left the hospital I had to go and get my car, but I'm pretty sure he doesn't care about that. Plus, I live to make Aiden's life as difficult as possible.

"I asked you a question," he says, following me.

"And I chose not to answer," I reply as I grab a bottle of water out of the fridge.

"Please tell me you haven't been out racing again. We can*not* take any more scandals."

"Of course not."

His shoulders drop.

"I picked up a prostitute and fucked her under the

Bean in front of all the tourists and hung the used condom from the goalpost at Soldier Field."

"Not. Funny."

I shrug. "How long have you been a pain in my ass? I thought you'd be used to it by now."

It's his turn to ignore me now.

"So, I spoke to the hospital about that boy you almost killed, and they said they expect him to make a full recovery. Unfortunately, the press *did* catch wind of your little… game, so we've released a statement, and you'll have to do a driver's ed course as well as a few hours' volunteer work at a road safety charity. No big deal."

"Seems like you've got everything under control, then."

He looks up from his phone. "Of course I do."

"Then why am I needed?"

"So I can express just how much effort I've put into cleaning up your mess. Oh, you're also paying the boy's hospital bills. The senator approved the withdrawal from your trust fund."

I nod. This I already knew, as I stopped by the billing department at the hospital before I left. "Fine. Can I go now?"

"No, you may not," the senator says as she waltzes in.

Senator Carla McLaughlin may look like a typical Midwest housewife, but I assure you, she's anything but.

She wears a Ralph Lauren shirt tucked into good ol' American Levi's, aiming for the upmarket-but-still-in-touch demographic.

"Senator," I sigh, taking a seat at the large kitchen island. For as long as I can remember, she has always been

"Senator." I think I called her mom once and was told in no uncertain terms to never do so again.

"Cavanaugh. I thought we talked about you and your reckless behavior?"

"We did, ma'am."

"So why is my chief of staff informing me about news that my son has gone and done something stupid? Again?"

"I don't know, ma'am."

"You don't know? How do you not know? Did someone else inhabit your body and do these things for you? Or do you have an evil twin running about that I do not know of and do not remember giving birth to?"

"No, ma'am."

"Then by all means, please explain to me why you once again put me in the difficult position of having to apologize for your actions?"

Yes, because this is all about her. Everything comes back to what it looks like to her constituents and the general voting public. "I let my anger get the better of me, and I did something stupid. There's no excuse for it; I can only seek to atone for my offensive behavior."

She nods and sips the coffee Aiden must have poured for her. "Good. There is a place in heaven for those who seek to redeem themselves, but you must first atone for your actions."

I nod.

"Has Aiden has told you the details of how we're going to fix this?" she asks.

"Yes, ma'am."

"Good." She puts down her cup as my father walks in.

Stewart McLaughlin looks like a man who handles his

own business, but that's as far as it goes. Tall, at six foot four, and solidly built with wide shoulders and a broad chest, he looks solid and capable but is meek as a kitten. He kisses the senator on the cheek and moves to the coffeepot.

"I just don't know where we went wrong with you," the senator says. "We gave you everything you ever wanted, raised you in a good, Christian home, and this is how you repay us?"

I want to explain I'm not *repaying* them for anything; I'm not even getting back at them for their overly strict ways. I'm just... a disappointment, I guess.

I can't, I won't, and will never be what they want me to be. I've tried, God knows I've tried, but I just... can't. So I guess I figure if I disappoint them in other ways first, maybe they won't be disappointed when I tell them I'm gay. Because I am. I'm done fighting it, I'm done hiding it, but I don't know if I'm *quite* ready for it all to come to an end just yet. Because it will. Despite me wanting them not to be disappointed, they will. Actually, they probably won't; they'll probably be livid before promptly kicking me out and publicly disowning me.

"All these problems with your behavior," the senator continues, "they're just not acceptable. I have an image to protect, a base to answer to. I can't be apologizing for you all the time, Cavanaugh, we've been through this."

"I know. I'm sorry."

"You are a senator's son, this isn't new to you, and yet you continually do these idiotic things." She throws her hands up. "I just... don't know what to do any more, Cavanaugh. You are such a disappointment to me. Your father and I would never have acted like this when we were your age. We respected our parents, obeyed them in everything. It is so confusing to me how your generation has no respect for anything! You could've killed that boy, and how would *that* look? We're lucky the sister has no interest in suing. That would've been the icing on the cake if she did." She turns to me. "I can*not* be put through a lawsuit, Cavanaugh. You know our name, my position make us targets for all sorts of frivolous claims. I will not open myself up to them."

I want to remind her I'm eighteen and that she's not responsible for my actions, but it's not worth it.

"Having said that, we have made the decision to cut you off. Even though you are eighteen, you are still financially dependent on us, which could lead to us being named as defendants in any lawsuit filed against you. And if you keep going as you are, there *will* be lawsuits."

Well, I didn't see this coming.

"We're moving you to the Streeterville property, which will be yours. We have paid your tuition until the end of the school year. Your college and trust funds will be released to you. You may take all your belongings and anything else you feel you may want. We will allow you a cook who will prep a week's worth of meals at a time, and a cleaner who will come in once a week. Their wages will come out of the ten million we'll give you to set you up. Thoughts?" she asks.

"Um...."

"It's really for the best," she says. "Publicly, nothing will change, of course. If people ask, we'll tell them you wanted a little more independence. You're eighteen, you'll be going off to college soon, it's not out of the ordinary. We do ask though that you *try* not to get into any more serious trouble. Even though we won't be liable for any lawsuits, it still doesn't look good for me to have to continually explain your behavior."

"Of course," I murmur, hearing but not really comprehending what's going on.

"Good, so it's all settled," the senator says, bouncing on her toes.

My father stays silent, while Aiden's smile could light up Sears Tower. "The movers will be here in two hours."

CHAPTER 9

Streeterville, according to all the people in the know, is one of Chicago's most luxurious suburbs. On the shore of Lake Michigan and in sight of Navy Pier, it's not hard to see why they think that.

Our, or now my, apartment is… nice, I guess. It's two floors, with massive glass walls to take advantage of the views. And now it's all mine.

I thank the movers and tip them generously for their efforts, although I guess I should be more mindful of my money, seeing as though it's mine?

The past few hours have been a blur. After I literally signed my life away, I packed up everything, and now here I am, in my own apartment, on my own.

I flop on the couch and look out over the vastness that is Lake Michigan.

What the fuck just happened? And what does this mean for me? It's a good thing, right? It means I can be who I want to be, doesn't it? I don't have to answer to my parents, even though I sort of do because I'm still a McLaughlin, but in name only.

I start laughing and can't stop.

This is all so fucked-up. Everything that's happened in the past twenty-four hours is fucked-up. First Connor, now this?

My laughter turns to tears. Tears for me, for my life, my future, for Connor, for us, if there ever can or will be an us.

I wake up to Helena, the cleaner, and Manuel, the chef, coming in to do their week's work.

"Oh, sorry, Mr. Cavanaugh," Helena says as I sit up.

I wave her off. "It's fine. How are you guys? Sorry for making you come all the way here."

Helena and Manuel have both worked for our family for years.

"Is okay," Manuel says as he drops a box of food on the kitchen bench. "We are getting paid extra."

Helena shushes him.

I laugh. "Good to know my, um, parents aren't stiffing you." The word "parents" gets stuck in my throat. Are they even my parents anymore? They've all but disowned me, haven't they? I mean, if they're parents in name only, they're not really parents, are they?

"You know your family treats us very good," Helena says.

"And you're worth every penny," I say as I get up and go to my room.

· · ·

When I emerge a couple of hours later, I find the two of them still here.

"Oh, I didn't realize you were still here," I say.

"Come, sit," Helena says, pulling out a stool at the kitchen bench.

Manuel puts a bowl of his famous French onion soup in front of me.

I take a spoonful of the creamy, onion-y goodness.

"Now, you want to tell us why we're all here?" Helena asks.

"My parents didn't tell you? I'll be going off to college next year, and I wanted to, um, spread my wings."

"And the real reason?" she asks, arching a brow.

My shoulders slump. "I, er, got in some, um, trouble again, and this was obviously the last straw."

"And they kicked you out."

I shake my head. "Senator McLaughlin would never do anything as uncouth as kicking her son out of the family home," I tell them. "They're disassociating from me."

"What that mean?" Manuel asks.

"That I'm basically on my own. Obviously I'm still a McLaughlin, but in name only. Oh, and in the eyes of the public, so I better not fuck up."

Helena and Manuel are speechless.

I shrug. "It's a liability thing. They don't want to be at risk of a lawsuit, you know, because it's an election year next year, and I guess I'm a—no, I know I'm a liability. This way they cut that." I dip my spoon into my soup, raise it, and dribble it back into the bowl.

Helena places her hand over the one of mine not

holding the spoon and ruining Manuel's soup. "You are not a liability."

I give her a half smile. "I kind of am." In more ways than one.

"Children are not liabilities," Manuel says. "Pains in the ass, yes, but not liability."

I chuckle. "Thanks, Manuel."

He waves me off and gives me more cheesy croutons.

"Your parents are wrong," Helena says.

"Are they?" I ask.

"*Yes*. It doesn't matter what you do or don't do, what you like or don't like, who you love," she says, giving me a pointed look. "Your parents are supposed to support you through it all."

I scoff. "Not mine. You know how important 'optics'"—I make air quotes—"are to the senator."

"Senator." She shakes her head. "It should be mom."

"She's never been Mom."

"No, she hasn't." She takes a breath and claps. "But now we can have fun, yes?"

"Fun?" My brow wrinkles.

"Yes. No more rules, no more anger, more *friends*." She bumps my shoulder when she says that.

"Helena, I don't know what you think you know, but I'm willing to bet you're wrong."

She tilts her head. "Am I?"

"Yes," I insist. "You are."

"Hmm, I think I am not."

"Helena…."

"It's not a problem for me, who you are. I see, you

know. I notice the girls you ignore. I know your parents would not approve, but…." She blows a raspberry.

I chuckle.

"The only thing that matters is that the person you love, loves you back and treats you good."

I nod, my throat thick.

"Maybe now you live here you can have… *friends* over."

"I'll cook!" Manuel exclaims.

We all laugh.

"I don't…. There's no one…. I…."

Helena squeezes my hand. "No rush. The option is always there, okay?"

I nod. "Thanks," I manage to choke out.

She pats my hand, gets up, and starts to clean up the mess Manuel made. Having Helena and Manuel's support is great and most definitely appreciated, but *it's not your parents,* a voice in my head says.

I know, I *know* I'll never get that from then, but I can't help but want it and maybe, just maybe, hope for it.

Having a gay son isn't the end of the world after all….

CHAPTER 10

The one good thing about living at home was that the drive to Windswept was only fifteen minutes. Now that I'm living in the heart of the city? It's triple that. But I do have to admit that when I drove out of the gates for the last time, it was a tiny bit easier to breathe.

That disappears when I drive through the gates of Windswept.

School is... almost worse than being at home. Here, not only do I have to live up to my parents' expectations, I have to live up to everyone else's parents' expectations. And it's always been this way. Yes, I'm Cavanaugh McLaughlin, but it's always the senator's son.

I walk into school with my usual I-don't-give-a-fuck swagger. The crowd parts as I walk by, the usual whispers rising in my wake. I know what they say. That I'm a bully, that I'm a murderer, that I rule the school. It's all noise. None of it matters, even if it is true.

My usual posse is waiting for me at my locker, desperate to be involved, to feel like I value their presence or friendship, that by association they too are "cool." As if any of that matters. They only want me because of my parents, because of who they think I'll be. They don't care that that's the furthest thing from my mind or that my parents are the scum of the earth.

No, they only care what I'll be able to do for them, now and into the future. None of them know me. None of them care to know me or about me.

"Yo, Cav!" Dan calls, holding his hand up for a high five.

I stare at it until he lowers it, a slight blush to his cheeks.

"How was your weekend? The Skids on Friday night was lit!"

There are a few chuckles from the group.

"But what happened afterward, man? You just ran. Did the cops catch up to ya?"

"Seriously, dude," Pete adds. "You guys just took off. Then we heard that there was an accident and like, Connor *died* or some shit."

"He didn't die," I snap.

Dan whacks Pete in the stomach. "Dude, there was an 'accident.'" He makes air quotes. "That's what we're calling it, hey, Cav?" He nudges me and gives me an exaggerated wink. "Because accidents are just accidents, but two deliberate acts equal a pattern."

"Two?" someone else, I don't know or care who, says. "What was the other one?"

"Duh, *Max*," another voice hisses.

"Shut up," a third voice says, but all eyes swing to me

to see how I'll react. Only the ignorant or the dumb mention Max in my presence.

"Get lost," I manage to grit out.

"But, Cav," Dan starts.

"Get the fuck away from me," I yell.

They all scatter, casting glances at me over their shoulders.

Max....

No one's mentioned him around me since it happened. Since I killed him.

Max was my first and I was his. I didn't mean for things to go as far as they did with him, but they did. Afterwards I did what I always do and leave. It must have been too much for Max and he snapped or something, I guess. I don't know. I got a call saying he'd gone crazy and had a gun so I got my ass back there. What I found.... *I* had done that to him. *I* forced him to that. I managed to pull him into the pool house where I tried to get the gun off him. And I did. I tried. But maybe I didn't try hard enough. And then I made it worse. I told him that we couldn't be together, that we would never be together, that I didn't want to be with him. It was the truth. Max was my friend but I wasn't in love with him. I wasn't even interested in him beyond our friendship. I didn't want to give him false hope. I didn't want to do that to him. I wanted to work things out between us, to help correct the mistake I made being with him. But he was too far gone in his own head. His last words before he pulled the trigger were "I'm nothing but a fuck up." The funny thing is, he wasn't the fuck up, *I* am. Maybe I always will be. The only thing Max fucked up was choosing to love me.

I still remember the warm spray of blood on my face and the sound of his body hitting the floor. I'll remember it every day for the rest of my life. And I deserve to. *I* slept with him knowing he was way more into me than I was to him. I knew he'd want more and I still went ahead with it. I didn't pull the trigger, but I may as well have.

There were so many rumors after Max died. Rumors about me. Rumors about him. Rumors about what he was saying. I wanted them all to stop. I *needed* them all to stop. So I did the only thing I could think of. I took ownership of all the misinformation that was going around. I used it to my advantage. No one is going to question someone who agrees they killed someone. Why would they? The senator, the CPD, the DA, they all knew the truth. The senator knew about my posturing but thought it was just that, posturing. She didn't know, would never know, it wasn't about making myself look bigger, badder. It was about the guilt I felt. The guilt I *still* feel.

But really, didn't I kill Max? I drove him to do it.

Maybe I am a black widow, doomed to maim or kill every guy who falls in love with me. It doesn't matter that Connor isn't dead or that I'm in love with him as well.

I shake my head, clearing the memories of the past, of past actions I can't fix, only to come face-to-face with Chloe Fontana.

CHAPTER 11

I've got to give the girl credit, she's got balls. She stands in front of me, all five foot two at a stretch, arms folded over the tits spilling out of her too-small blouse. Her eyes are narrowed, foot tapping on the floor. The hallway has emptied out, the bell obviously long gone.

"Can I help you?" I ask. Even though we've been in school together since kindergarten, I honestly haven't had much, if anything, to do with Chloe. From what I gather, she's a cool chick. A little angry and a lot standoffish, but I can respect that.

"What did you do to Connor?" she demands.

I lean against my locker. "I didn't do anything to him."

"Then why the fuck is he in hospital with a hole in his lung and missing a spleen?"

"Because he's a shit driver who couldn't spot the car coming from the opposite direction."

She slams me up against the wall. "And why did he fail to see the other car? What were you doing to distract him?"

I scoff. "I wasn't doing anything."

"I suppose he's just another mark on your tally, huh? Just like Max Emory."

I smack her hands away from me. "You have something you want to say to me?"

She shakes her head. "Okay, I'll be straight with you. I'm Connor's best friend, aside from Jase. He may think he's slick and hid whatever the fuck is going on between you two, but he didn't."

I swear my heart stops in my chest.

She takes a breath. "Look, I'm not going to say anything. It's not my place to out you, but if you continue to hurt him, I promise you, I *will* make your life unpleasant indeed."

I chuckle, both at her threat and her moxie. "Sweetheart, I'm the gay son of a conservative senator. What makes you think you can make my life even more unpleasant than it already is?" I don't know why I can admit I'm gay. I don't know why it's her I can admit it to, either. But I can't deny it feels good to do so. I'm still a long way from shouting it over the loudspeaker at Wrigley Field like I know Thomas would want me to do, but baby steps.

Her shoulders drop.

I move so I'm pressing against her. "And just so you know, it's *killing* me Connor is hurt and in hospital because of me."

"Oh," she says.

"But that's between us, okay?"

She nods. I don't know why I said that to her. For all I

know, she could blab to the whole school what I just told her, but something tells me she won't.

"Good." I start to walk away, but she grabs my arm, stopping me.

"Do you care about him?" she asks.

"A hell of a lot more than I should," I admit.

She nods. "He's a good guy."

"I know."

"You're not."

"No, I'm not," I agree. "But neither is Thomas." Am I throwing my friend under the bus? Yes, but something tells me this isn't news to Chloe.

"He's also not gay or panbread or whatever he's claiming to be."

I chuckle. I like this girl. "No, he's not."

"So why then is he sticking his tongue down Connor's throat every chance he gets?"

I shift my weight from foot to foot.

"He's using Connor to get to you, isn't he?"

"How'd you know?"

She shrugs. "Lucky guess. I see the way you look at Connor. I see the way Thomas looks at you. Spoiler alert, they're not at all the same."

I chuckle. I like this girl.

"Thomas has been jealous of you for years, but you've either been too blind or too dumb to notice. Unfortunately, I can't say the same of him. He's smart, I'll give him that."

"He got one thing right. Let's not pretend he's MENSA worthy."

"Yeah, but he's got you by the balls, doesn't he?" She tilts her head. "Although you might like that."

This time I full-on laugh. "You're one hell of a piece of work," I say, slinging my arm around her shoulders. "I love it."

She shrugs. "A girl's gotta get her kicks somehow."

"Oh, I get the impression that you don't have any trouble getting your kicks."

"Not usually," she admits. "But when they just happen to fall in my lap? Then it's even better."

We continue to walk down the hall for a bit, neither of us in a rush to get to class.

"So," she says eventually, "what are we going to do about your BFF?"

"Do?" I ask.

"Yeah. I mean, he is with your guy, right?"

"I'm working on it," I tell her.

"But you'll have something soon?"

I run a hand over my head. "I-I...."

She stops and stares at me, hands on her hips. "What the fuck, dude?"

"Thomas wants me to come out," I tell her. "Probably in some grand fucking spectacle, humiliating me and my parents in the process." Even though my parents have more than proved they don't give a shit about me, I'm still their son.

"Oh. Shit," she says.

I nod. "Yeah. I want to be with Connor; I do. I want him *so* badly, but I can't do that."

She nods. "So Thomas continues on his evil way."

"For the moment." I take a breath. "I just need time. That's all."

She threads her arm through mine, and we keep walking.

"You really want to be with him, huh?"

I nod. "Yeah, I do."

"So what happened on Friday?"

I blow out a breath. "I let everything get to me, and Connor was caught in the crosshairs." I shake my head. "I'd do anything to take it back, or even swap places with him."

"You love him," she says.

I shrug.

"Cav...."

"Look, I'm working on it, okay? I don't feel like I'm in a place to do anything right now, no matter how much I want to, but I'm working on it. Not all of our lives are sunshine and rainbows."

She nods. "Okay."

"I have a legacy and a reputation to protect." I go on for no other reason than I feel I have to justify myself to her, even though I know I don't. "My whole world is probably going to come crumbling down. That's a big deal."

"I know," she agrees. "But it won't be your whole world. You'll have Connor—and me—if you want it."

I look down at the usually worked-up spitfire and smile. Her expression mirrors mine.

"Thank you."

"You're welcome. But you do realize that until that time, we have to be mortal enemies."

I throw my head back and laugh. "Mortal enemies?"

"Hey, I'm just keeping your cover intact."

"Were we ever mortal enemies?" I ask.

"No, but you're pretending to hate Connor, so…."

I nod.

"I don't actually know if we've ever had a proper conversation," she continues.

I stop and think. "I don't think we have either."

"When you let people underneath that hard exterior, you're not actually a bad guy, Cavanaugh McLaughlin."

I look around the empty hall. "Shhh, someone might hear you."

She laughs.

"Not that I believe that to be true, but thanks for the sentiment."

She stops me with a hand on my forearm. "You're a good guy in a situation that's forcing you to be a not-so-good guy. The good news is it isn't permanent."

Down the end of the hall, a door opens and Jase steps out. He looks up and sees us, his eyes narrowing when he realizes who I am.

It may not be permanent, but it is going to be a lot of work to undo.

CHAPTER 12

It's funny how much has changed away from school, but in it? It's like nothing has happened at all.

I take my usual seat at our table, my "friends" barely reacting to my presence. I don't know if that's a good thing or a bad one.

"Where's Thomas?" I ask, looking around. It should've occurred to me before now that he's not here, but it didn't.

"He's, uh, not here," Pete says eventually.

"Where is he?"

"I, um, assume he's at the hospital, you know, with, um, Connor."

"Yeah, the fairy has to hold his 'boyfriend's'"—Dan makes air quotes—"hand while he gets better." He turns to me. "Tell me, how much are you paying Thomas to play gay, huh? Must be some serious dough. I mean, why else would he be doing all this? He's gotta get something out of it and there's no *way* Thomas would be doing this out of the goodness of his own heart."

"I don't know," Pete says, "he genuinely seems to care for him. Maybe he's like, bi or some shit?"

"Why would you think I'm paying him?" I ask.

There are nervous murmurings.

"Er, because why else would he be doing what he's doing?" Pete asks.

"I mean, surely Thomas wouldn't be stupid enough to go against *you*," Dan mumbles.

I have to hold back my eye roll.

"Or is he there to finish the job?"

I smash my hands on the tabletop.

Jase shakes his head as he walks past our table. "You're a joke," he says.

"Jase…." I start.

He holds up a hand. "Don't. Until you can man up, just don't."

"Do you know who you're talking to?" Pete asks. "Cav is plenty manly."

Jase folds his arms across his chest. "If that's the case why hasn't he manned up?"

Dan chortles. "Did you not see what he did to your brother? He manned up plenty."

"And then there's Thomas," Jase adds.

"Exactly." Dan says. "And now he has Thomas to finish off. Why should Cav get his hands dirty when he can get someone else to do it for him? Besides, it's not like Connor's that important that he'd risk going down for it."

Jase looks at me. "Not important. Is that what Connor is to you?"

"What else would he be?" Dan answers for me.

"I don't know, Cav, what else could Connor be?"

"Well, he could be roadkill," someone says.

My head snaps to the side, but not before I see Jase's eyes blaze.

"What did you say?" I demand.

There's awkward glances and nervous shuffling.

"I'm going to tell you all once and once only. I'm the only one who can talk shit about Connor Siddell, okay?"

Jase scoffs and shakes his head. "Because God forbid someone else does."

I ignore him. "Are we clear?"

There are murmurs in response.

"I said, are we clear?"

"Yes, Cav," they mumble.

"You're a joke," Jase says.

I grab his arm and drag him out of the cafeteria. I walk us to a small AV room and close the door.

"What the fuck, Cav?" he says, rubbing his arm.

"What did you expect me to do, huh?" I ask. "I have a reputation to protect, and you're actively trying to undermine that." Coming out to Chloe is one thing, but totally doing a 180 in front of everyone? It's not something I'm *quite* ready for. But I can't have Jase undermining me, questioning me. I want to do this on my own time.

"Because you're an ass."

I sit on the one desk in the small room. "But you've always known that. You don't actually think I'm friends with you because I genuinely like you, do you?"

He shuffles his feet.

"I'm friends with you because I wanted to piss your brother off."

"I thought…."

"That what? Because I love your brother that I'd change all of a sudden?"

His head shoots up when I mention I'm in love with Connor.

To be honest, I like Jase. He's a cool kid but naïve as fuck. I know he's been through a lot and Connor sheltered him as much as he could, but he didn't do the kid any favors in doing so.

But all this means nothing here. I have a reputation to protect, and I can't have anyone fucking with it.

"You love Connor?"

"Look, it's irrelevant at this point—"

"But it's not," he interrupts. "You *love* my brother, and I'm pretty sure the feeling is mutual."

I don't want to explore what my heart does when he says that, but I can't ignore the way it squeezes.

"I don't—"

"You do," Jase insists.

"Whatever. He's with Thomas."

"And whose fault is that?" He folds his arms across his chest.

"To be fair, I didn't directly have anything to do with them getting together. If they got together in order to piss me off or whatever, that's on them."

There's no reaction from Jase.

I blow out a breath. "Look, I'm an asshole, the worst person on the planet. This isn't news."

"I suppose," Jase concedes.

"And it's not like I'm not paying for this. I'm the one

who has to watch the guy I love prance around with a guy who would quite happily watch me burn."

"Yeah, that's gotta suck for you."

I chuckle. "Just a bit."

"So what are you going to do about it?" he asks.

My shoulders sag. "I need time. From *everyone*," I say. "There's a lot more at stake for me than just coming out and living happily ever after with Connor. As much as I want that to be the case." I run a hand over my head. "Then there's the wrath my parents are going to rain down on us. I wouldn't wish that on anyone."

"Oh, please," Jase says, rolling his eyes. "Spare me the martyr act. You know Connor isn't into Thomas. And I know you know it because I just fucking told you, as well as all the rest of it. As for Thomas, your best friend may just have you beat for the world's biggest asshole. He's jealous of you. He's happy to take the fame and power that comes with being your friend, but he wants his own. He's sick of being in your shadow. He's found a weakness of yours and he's going to exploit it every chance he gets. He won't ever stop until he gets what he wants."

I nod. I know Thomas won't stop, but like I said, I need time. I'm getting there. Talking to Chloe is a prime example, but I feel safe with her. But everyone else? How are they going to react? After everything I've said? After everything I've done? Cavanaugh McLaughlin, your number one hypocrite right here.

"You *know* he doesn't love Connor," he presses. "You *know* Connor doesn't love him, so what are you going to do?"

"I... I...."

He shakes his head. "Seriously?"

"It's not so easy!" I yell. "Connor deserves someone who can show him off, someone who doesn't need to hide their relationship. I can't give that to him."

"So you're going to let him go? Just like that?"

"My parents… they wouldn't approve. It would be devastating to the senator's campaign, her reputation, her standing with the party, with her constituents." Doing things here and there to piss off Aiden is one thing. Taking responsibility for Max's death is another, although I have a feeling she thinks that's just my teenage rebellion. But to come out and live a life the opposite to everything she stands for? It's a lot.

"So the alternative is you being miserable and alone for the rest of your life?"

I shrug, my hands slapping my legs.

"Cav… you can't live like that," he says.

"I know." Pressure builds behind my eyes. I blink to make the tears disappear, but all it does is make one fall. I look up. "You want to know something funny?"

He nods.

"My parents kicked me out yesterday. Made me sign a thing saying they're no longer responsible for me. They don't want to be named in a lawsuit in case I kill someone or do something equally idiotic."

He comes over to me and pats my shoulder. I hadn't noticed before, but he and Connor smell the same. "So why are you still protecting them?" he asks.

"They're my parents," I say. "I mean, they've never really been like, supportive or loving or anything but…."

"But they're the ones who raised you."

"Yeah."

He sighs. "Look, I get wanting to have something you can't have. I'd give anything to have even an hour more with my parents, but there comes a time where you have to move on. It's not healthy to keep holding on to the past or hoping for a future that's never going to eventuate."

I nod. "I know. It's stupid. They couldn't be clearer that they don't give a shit about me. I should just cut all ties with them altogether."

"If you think there's a possibility that they'd change their minds—"

"There isn't," I say, cutting him off.

"Oh."

I chuckle. "I don't know. Maybe I'm a coward. Maybe I'm always going to be a scared little boy who's hoping his mommy and daddy notice him, that they take an interest in him past what he can do for their image. That would be the smart thing to do."

"You know I'm here if you need anything, right?" he asks. "I know Connor would be too."

"Thanks, Jase. And for what it's worth, I really am sorry about being such an asshole."

"It's all right."

"No, it's not."

He laughs. "No, it isn't, but you can make it right if you want to. You know, when you're ready."

"Thanks. How is Connor anyway? I should've asked you that before."

"I think I would've decked you if you had." He chuckles. "But he's okay. Still has a headache and is sore, but he'll live."

I nod as the bell rings. "That's good. I'm glad to hear it."

Jase heads to the door. "He was asking about you, too. He said he thought he remembered hearing your voice but can't remember when or what you said."

I give him a sad smile. "Tell him it was a dream."

CHAPTER 13

In the end, Thomas was out for a week. I have no idea what he was doing during that time. I'm fairly certain he wasn't at the hospital though.

But when he came back, he had the worried boyfriend bit down to an art. And he made sure to come and sit with us so I would know all about it.

"It was full on," he tells our "friends." "His spleen was ruptured, so they had to take it out, and his rib was broken and had punctured his lung. That's some serious shit."

There are nods and exclamations all around.

"Thank God he's okay, I was *so* worried."

I can't help but snort into my orange Gatorade.

I earn a side-eye from Thomas, but come on! He's laying it on *way* too thick. Not that he lets that stop him.

"There's just something that transforms a relationship when you've been through such a tragic event like this. I mean, I could've lost him, he could've *died*. Then where would I be, you know? I mean, this guy is my one true love—"

This time Gatorade comes shooting out my nose. "Sorry," I splutter.

"There a problem, Cavanaugh?" Thomas asks. He arches an eyebrow, daring me to say something.

I clear my throat. "Why would there be a problem, Thomas?" I counter.

"Dude," Dan says. "Lay off the gay talk. You know how uncomfortable it makes Cav."

"Yes," Thomas agrees. "It makes him *so* uncomfortable." He pauses. "My apologies."

"But I mean, we're also glad Connor's okay," Dan adds. Cocksucker.

"He's definitely on the mend, and at least now he's out of the hospital. His sister Amy has been *so* sweet, too. We've really become great friends since the accident. I mean, I'm practically living with them; I'm there all the time. She doesn't mind a bit."

"I'm sorry, what?" I ask.

"Oh yeah," Thomas says. "Me and Amy, we've really bonded this past week. She's really supportive of Connor and me and doesn't mind that I'm over there as much as I am."

"So you two are like, almost shacking up then," Pete says.

Thomas shrugs. "Pretty much. I want to be there for every step of his recovery and that means I have to be where he is. I mean, I tried to get him to move into my place, but he didn't want to impose."

I have to stop from rolling my eyes. How can Amy be

so blind? How can she fall for his tricks? And does Connor like him being there? He's obviously made no moves to get him to stop coming around, so what does *that* mean? Does he still want Thomas? Does he not want me anymore?

"In love and basically living together," Dan states. "So when's the wedding?"

I crush the plastic bottle in my hand.

"Shit, sorry, Cav," Dan says, looking at the table.

Thomas's expression says the exact opposite.

"What's this about Thomas practically moving in with Connor?" I say to Chloe as she swaps her books at her locker.

"Hi, Cav, how are you? I'm great, thanks for asking."

"Whatever. Thomas moving in with Connor," I say again.

"I honestly think Connor had very little to do with this," she says. "And when I mean very little, I mean like, nothing to do with this."

"So why's it happening then?"

"Because it just did. According to Connor, Thomas kept coming around, and kept coming around, and kept coming around, even though Connor told him he didn't want him to."

"So they're still together?" I ask.

She shrugs. "I guess. It's obvious to me and anyone with half a brain that Connor's not into it, like, at all, but he hasn't pulled that particular trigger just yet. And even if he did...."

"And even if he did, what?" I ask.

She blows out a breath. "I don't know if Thomas would actually listen to what Connor was saying. The fact that he's practically living with them now says all you need to know about his comprehension skills."

I run a hand over my head.

"And then there's Amy," she continues.

"What about Amy?"

She sighs. "She's bought into Thomas's act hook, line, and sinker. *That's* why Thomas is around so much, because Amy lets him. She thinks the sun shines out of his ass and that he's good for Connor."

"Unlike me who put him in the hospital in the first place."

"Well, yeah, probably."

She grabs my arm. "Look, I honestly don't think you have too much to worry about. Thomas and Connor aren't doing anything. Connor's in no shape to argue with anyone right now."

"How is he?" I ask.

"He's okay. Concussion's gone, with no lingering effects, and he's healing from the surgery."

I blow out a breath. "Good."

"You know, you could ask him yourself. I know he's been asking about you."

"He doesn't need to be worrying about me."

"Yet, he is. I know you think you're doing the right thing, but you're not."

I sigh. "I know, but what can I do?"

"I don't know, maybe pick up the phone and talk to the guy? He wants to hear from you."

"Trust me, he doesn't want to know what I have to say."

"I'm pretty sure he does, but whatever. You know best." She rolls her eyes.

I grab her shoulder and spin her to face me. "I *do* know better. I'm not good for him. Look at where he is, what he's recovering from."

"And yet, he's still asking for you. Look, you obviously care very deeply for him. I know you think you're protecting him, that he deserves better than you, but all you're doing is forcing him into decisions and situations you have no right to."

"How is it fair for me to take him, claim him, when I can't do any of that publicly?" I ask. "I can't hold his hand when we walk down the halls, I can't take him out for deep dish or to a baseball game. How fair is that for him?"

"How fair is it to either of you for you to be miserable?" she hits back. "What you two have is special, something that you don't find every day. Are you willing to risk that because you're afraid or you think he deserves better? Isn't that for him to decide?"

"I don't want to hurt him again."

"So don't."

"You say that like it's simple."

"Why isn't it? People do it every day."

"I'm not a normal person."

"No, you're an asshole, but a caring one."

"Thomas has practically moved into his house."

"And people can't move out?" she asks. "Show Amy who Thomas really is, I bet she'll change her tune like that." She snaps her fingers. "Or better yet, show her and

Connor, just how much you care for him. It's a coldhearted bitch who would deny true love."

I roll my eyes at her phrasing. "He's still recovering. Plus, he and Amy are finally getting along. I don't want to fuck that up for him."

"You won't fuck it up! Stop thinking you're going to ruin everything!"

"But that's what I do."

"For fuck's sake." She throws up her hands. "I know you think you do, but I'm here to tell you, you're not *that* much of a fuck up."

"My parents kicked me out," I tell her. I don't know why I tell her, or what it has to do with the conversation we're currently having, but I guess I needed to tell someone and Chloe is it.

"What?"

I shuffle my feet. "I guess they saw me as a liability on top of being a publicity nightmare so they, um, like, all but publicly disowned me. They gave me our Streeterville penthouse, and I'm, um, living on my own."

"Holy shit."

I shrug.

"Do they know…. Have you told them…?" Chloe trails off.

"That I'm gay?" Saying it here with Chloe isn't a problem. And the more times I say it to her, the easier it gets, but the thought of coming out to my parents? Scares the shit out of me.

She nods.

"Ha! There's no way they would've given me the apartment if they knew that. Not that that's the reason I haven't told them." I scramble to explain myself. "I mean, I didn't not do it just so I could get the apartment, but you know...."

She nods. "Coming out to your parents, it's... well, it's not the easiest thing to do, especially with parents like ours."

"Yeah."

"But they're still your parents. Even if they have kicked you out, it's not so easy to give up on them."

"No, it's not." I have to say, it's so refreshing to be able to talk to someone who understands what I'm going through.

She shrugs. "But it still has to be done."

"I know."

"And not just so you can get Connor."

I roll my eyes.

"Is Thomas being good to him?" I ask. I hate how small my voice is, but I can't help it. This whole thing... it's killing me.

"Thomas is good to him," she says. "He's also annoying the shit out of him but it is what it is."

I nod.

"But is good really good enough for Connor?" she asks.

"If it's what he needs. He's with his family. A family who love him. I know how valuable that is. I can't even be with him in public for fuck's sake."

"But at least he'd be with you," she points out.

"A closeted me."

"What happens if he thinks that's better than whatever the fuck you two have got going on now?" she asks.

"Then I'd say he's either on some seriously good pain meds or is seeing things through 'everything is champagne and butterflies' glasses. I live in the real world where not everyone gets their happily ever after."

"Annnnnnnnnnd he's back," she says.

"I never went anywhere," I retort, walking away.

CHAPTER 14

The next day, Thomas catches up with me as I park my car.

"I noticed you didn't take your usual route home yesterday."

I repress my groan. The last thing I need is for him to know what's happening with me and my parents. "Maybe I felt like taking the scenic route."

"Hmmm, no, I don't think that's it."

I lean against my car. "Then why don't you tell me what you think it is?"

He starts pacing in front of me. "I think someone is in the doghouse with Senator Mommy Dearest and is hiding out, waiting for the storm to blow over."

"Oh you do, do you?"

"It's my favorite theory."

"So there's more?" I ask.

"Yeah, but each more unlikely than the one before it."

I nod and push off the car. "Cool."

"So what is it?" he asks, falling into step with me as I walk into school.

"You're already got it figured out. Why do you need me? I deny it, you're not going to believe it, I confirm it, and you already knew."

"You think you're clever, don't you?"

"Clearly not as clever as you are, but I think I'm up there."

"So the senator's not real happy with you, huh?"

I stop to face him again. "What are you doing, Thomas?" I ask.

He clutches his chest. "I can't be concerned about my friend?"

I snort. "So we're friends again now? I don't think so."

He grabs my arm and pulls me to a stop. "I was your friend. I still am. I always will be. I can't believe you'd even doubt that."

"Gee, I wonder why I would?" I always knew Thomas was a little cuckoo, but this, this is hitting new lows.

"Is this about Connor? Because I'm not going to apologize for falling in love with him." I have no idea why he's laying it on so thick with me when he doesn't need to. I know exactly why Thomas is doing what he's doing, and it's not because he's in love with Connor.

"So you're telling me you truly love him?" I ask. I want to see just how far he's going to stick to this line.

"Of course I do."

I nod. "What do you love about him?"

"What do you mean?"

"I mean, what are the things you love most about him?

Does he secretly nerd out to *Pokémon* or does he love *Avatar: The Last Airbender*? Does he eat in a super specific way? Does he only drink a certain drink? Is he super embarrassing when he watches sport, or does he sing some lame 2000s-era pop punk band's songs in the shower?"

He looks to the ground and stubs it with his Gucci loafer. "Um...."

"That's what I thought," I say and start walking again.

I only get a few feet before he grabs me again. "You think this proves anything?" he asks.

"No, I know it doesn't. I knew your relationship was bullshit from the start."

"You forced me to do this," he hisses.

"I never did anything. You did. All of this, it's all you."

He nods and crosses his arms over his chest. "Yeah, that's right. It *is* all about me. For once. For once I've got the great Cavanaugh McLaughlin by the balls. How does it feel?"

"It feels pretty shitty, to be honest," I say.

"Yeah, that's right. It's time you got a taste of your own medicine. Do you know how hard it is to constantly be in your shadow?" he asks.

"Who's asked you to?" I shoot back. "I have always treated you as an equal."

He scoffs. "Yeah, being your errand boy is really being treated as an equal."

I pinch the bridge of my nose. "That's how we're going to play it?" I ask.

"That's how it *was*," he insists.

"Because that's how you wanted it!" I yell. "You never

wanted to take the lead on anything, you *always* deferred to me. What was I supposed to do?"

"I never—"

"Yes, you did. You never had the balls to go after what you wanted. You sat back and watched me, let me do all the hard work, and you swooped in afterwards. I did what I had to. I have *always* done what I had to. What have you done?"

"I've cleaned up your mess—"

"You mean you've profited from them."

"I've supported you—"

"In public. In private you've done everything you can to undermine me."

He shrugs and examines his fingernails. "After a while I figured, why not have some fun? Why let you get all the good stuff? At first it was fun, picking up all the girls you left behind at whatever function you were at, giving information on the senator to the papers, her opposition, whoever, but even that gets old."

"So you moved on to Connor."

"It was perfect. I mean, you basically set it up yourself. When it comes to who you like to stick your dick in, I figured out fairly early what your type was. The girls who have escorted you to whatever were the finest of the fine, man, and you threw them away! Didn't even give them a second look. That was a travesty."

I shake my head and laugh. "You're something else."

"I'm an opportunist is what I am, and right now I have the *biggest* opportunity of my life." He steps closer to me. "Not only do I know your secret, I have the one person you'd be willing to risk it all for. And that makes me one powerful motherfucker right now."

"So what are you going to do about it?" I ask. On one hand, I thought Thomas was my friend. On the other, we haven't been close like we used to be for a while. There's also the grudging acknowledgment that he might have a point about how I treated him in the past.

"I hadn't thought about it," he says, turning and continuing up the stairs.

"Bullshit," I spit, following him.

"Maybe I'll sit and let you stew for a bit, make you experience a bit of what I went through, even if it is only a fraction. Or maybe I'll go to the senator and Mr. McLaughlin with what I know. Or maybe I'll bypass that altogether and go straight to the *Sun Times*. The possibilities are endless."

With that, he turns and walks into the building.

CHAPTER 15

onnor: You're avoiding me.

I sigh as I read his message. I was wondering how long it would take him to start.

Connor: And now you're ignoring me.

I flop back on my bed.

Connor: I'd send you a nude but I think my bandages might ruin the effect.

Connor: Please, Cav, just talk to me.

Connor: Please.

My heart is begging me to respond, even if it is just to tell him to fuck off.

My head is telling me not to take the bait. That this is a slippery slope and opening the door to him now will only make things harder.

I stay strong.

But Connor, not having received a response to any of his texts, starts calling.

I let it go to voicemail.

There's silence for a minute before he calls again.

Again, I let it go to voicemail.

The pattern repeats five more times.

Connor: You can ignore me all you want, but I'll keep calling, keep filling your voicemail with meaningless messages.

Cav: Please, just leave me alone.

Connor: He speaks!

Cav: I'm serious, Connor. Leave me alone.

Connor: What happens if I don't want to?

Connor: What happens if I can't?

Cav: You're with Thomas. The way he tells it, he's practically living with you.

Connor: Only because he won't leave! I've tried and tried and tried but he won't get the message.

Cav: But you still let it happen in the first place.

Connor: I was, and still am, on some pretty sweet pain meds. I'm sure a lot of things happened without me knowing about it. But I have asked him to leave. Several times.

Connor: I also had my spleen removed and am recovering from a punctured lung, so any resistance is relative.

Cav: I'm sorry.

Connor: I'm alive. I'll heal.

Cav: Not just about that.

Connor: Fuck this. Will you please answer my call?

Connor: Cav?

Connor: Please.

Connor: We need to talk.

Connor: Answer your fucking phone, McLaughlin

He follows that up with several angry face emojis.

Cav: Ok

"Fucking finally," he says when I answer.

"Now will you leave me alone?" I ask.

"We need to talk," he says.

"And we have. Good—"

"About actual things, not just hearing each other's voice."

"We shouldn't be doing this."

"Says who? We're just fucking talking."

"Mph."

"And quit acting like your heart isn't bursting out of your chest to hear my voice," he says.

"It's not." It totally is.

"Uh-huh, *sure*."

"Well? You wanted to talk, so talk."

He snickers. "Hi, Connor, how are you? How are your injuries? Are you in pain? Is there anything I can do for you?"

It's my turn to chuckle.

"I'm okay, for the record," he says.

"Good. I'm, um, glad."

"Don't sound so enthusiastic."

I sigh. "What do you want from me, Connor?"

"You know, while I was in the hospital I had a very lovely nurse looking after me. Very kind, very talkative. She made passing the time a lot easier."

"And what? You fell in love with her and are leaving Thomas so the two of you can run off into the sunset together?"

Connor laughs. "Nope. Still very firmly in the 'I like guys' camp."

"So why do I care about this nurse?"

"Because Shelly, her name is Shelly by the way, had some very interesting stories to tell."

My stomach drops. She wouldn't dare, would she? "She's a nurse in a busy Chicago hospital. I'm sure she's full of interesting stories."

"That's probably true, but the stories that were of particular interest to me featured one Cavanaugh McLaughlin."

"How did she find out my last name?" I ask.

"Aha!" he cries. "So you *do* know her."

"What? No. I was just, um, wondering how some random nurse knows me."

"She knows you because, according to her, you displayed some very loving behavior."

"Sounds like someone's been dipping into the Oxy."

"Or someone's trying to hide things from me they don't want me to know."

I stay silent.

"I remember hearing your voice," he tells me. "You know, after the accident."

"I pulled you out of your car; of course you heard my voice. I was trying to make sure you hadn't done something stupid like kill yourself."

"It's okay to be worried about me, you know." I can hear the smile in his voice.

"Is it?" I ask.

"Of course it is."

"Why? I mean, we're not dating, we're not even friends, so why is it okay that I was worried about you?"

"Ignoring the fact that you admitted you *were* worried

about me, it's okay to admit you care about people, Cav. It's okay you care about *me*."

I sigh. "I can't be worried about you, Connor."

"Then don't," he says. "Don't be worried about me. Don't pull me out of wrecked cars, don't hold my hand in ambulances, don't sit by my bedside, don't visit me when you think I'm sleeping. Don't call me or text me or do anything. Just leave me alone."

My heart squeezes. "I can't do that either," I whisper.

"Fuck, Cav."

"I'm sorry," I say. "I shouldn't have answered your call. This was a mistake."

"Don't," he tells me. "Don't pull back from me again."

"I—"

"Please, Cav," he begs. "I can't take it, not again."

"This, us, is never going to happen," I warn him.

"Says who?"

"God, fate, me. Take your pick."

"And I say to all three of you that you can go fuck yourselves."

I chuckle. "Bold move, telling someone who controls your future to go fuck themselves."

"It's not much of a future without you, so what does it matter?"

"Connor...."

"Enough of this bullshit, Cav. I want to be with you, and despite what you say, I know you want to be with me too. I'm willing to wait, baby. As long as you give me some sort of timeframe to work with, some sort of assurance that at some stage we will be together in public then I'll wait."

I stay silent.

"I know your family situation is complicated—"

"Ha!" That's the understatement of the century.

"But," he continues, "the time has come where you have to decide which way you want your life to go. You can't hide forever. You shouldn't *have* to hide forever. You need to make a choice here, Cav. Are you content to do everything your parents want and expect of you, or do you want to live your life your way?"

"They kicked me out," I tell him. "Not because I'm gay, but because they're worried you or Amy or someone else I hurt in a race will sue them."

"So why are you still playing their game?" he asks.

"I…." I trail off. The truth is, I don't know. They're my parents, but it's clear they don't love me, and I don't owe them any loyalty.

"They don't want what's best for you, Cav," he says. "Do they even care?"

I blow out a breath.

"I don't want to be that guy, the one forcing you to come out and do anything you're not ready for but—"

"But you're hearing all this and you're wondering why the hell I'm still playing the part," I finish for him.

"Well, yeah."

I nod. "It's a fair question."

"Do you have an answer for me?" he asks.

"Not one that makes sense."

He blows out a breath.

"But I do have a question for you," I tell him.

"Go on."

"You're sitting there, telling me I should get myself out

from underneath my parents' thumb, but what about you?"

"Me?"

"Yes, you."

"What do I have to do with any of this?"

"Not this specifically, but you have your own problem." To be honest, I'm kind of amazed he hasn't figured it out already.

"And what problem would that be?"

"Who's living in your house right now?" I ask. "Who's in your bed?"

"He's in a guest bed," he says.

"But who's there?" I ask again.

"I didn't have a choice," he explains. "When I was discharged, Thomas was here waiting for me, bags packed and everything. There was nothing I could do."

"So you don't know how to call the cops?" I ask. "Tell them you have someone illegally squatting in your house? And what about Jase? I can't imagine he's happy to have Thomas there twenty-four seven."

He's silent.

"I'm not the only one with a problem and a situation that doesn't make sense."

"Thomas isn't anything to me," he finally says.

"Then why are you still with him?" I ask. "Surely a relationship that doesn't mean anything to you would be easier to break than mine with my parents."

"You want me to break up with Thomas?"

"I want you to do whatever the fuck you want," I say, despite the opposite being true. "I was simply pointing out the hypocrisy, that's all."

"Say I end things with him, does that mean you'll come out to your parents?"

"Is that what you want?"

"Yes," he says. Steadfast. Confident. Demanding. My dick jerks in my jeans.

"You don't play fair."

"I never said I did."

"Looks like we're at an impasse then," I say.

"Looks like we are," he agrees.

"Then let the best man win."

CHAPTER 16

For the next week, Thomas let me stew.

The only good thing was that I got plenty of updates on Connor, who was recovering well, a doting Thomas by his side. I was inundated with a plethora of needling comments, all designed to push my buttons. It was working.

"It's so nice to be feel helpful and wanted," Thomas says one day at lunch. "It gives you a real sense of purpose, you know?"

"You watch," someone says, "he's gonna become a doctor now."

There's hysterical laughter.

"I think I'll stick to playing naughty nurse," he says, wriggling his eyebrows.

"You're into cross dressing?" Dan asks.

Thomas smacks the back of his head. "Men can be nurses too, you fuck."

I want, desperately, to ask if Connor is up to that, but I can't.

Thomas looks over at me, smiles, and blows me a kiss.

I thump my fists against the tabletop.

Everyone stops.

"Enough," I say.

"Problem?" Thomas asks, batting his eyelashes at me.

"I don't want to hear all this gay boy shit while I eat my lunch." My stomach roils as the words come out of my mouth.

Thomas leans back. "I thought you'd be happy to hear the guy you almost killed was okay. But then, killing someone isn't new to you, is it?"

I lean back. "That's right, it's not. I'm also not afraid to add to my tally either." I raise my eyebrows at him.

The other guys laugh and catcall while Thomas sits and stares.

Even though it was my decision to take responsibility for Max's death, it still cuts me every time someone mentions it. But that is my penitence. It's my punishment for being there, for forcing his hand. I couldn't give Max what he wanted, what he needed. I couldn't be what he needed me to be. But I can take that lesson and learn from it.

"What? Haven't you hurt Connor enough already?" Thomas asks.

"I was talking about you," I tell him.

There's a chorus of "ooooooooohs."

"Um, guys?" Pete asks.

Thomas holds his hand up. "This is how it's going to be?" he asks me.

I shrug. "You tell me."

He smiles and nods. "Okay."

"Okay," I repeat.

"Ah, does someone want to tell us what the fuck just happened?" Dan asks.

Thomas smacks his cheek a couple of times. "Don't worry your pretty little head about it, Danny boy."

He shakes his head. "You guys are fucking weird lately."

"Don't worry about it," I tell him.

"I mean, like what's going on? Are you guys friends? Not friends? Frenemies? What?"

"Frenemies?" Thomas asks, chuckling.

"I said don't worry about it," I repeat, despite the fact I don't actually know the answer to that question. I don't really care to, either.

Thomas has something I want. He also knows a secret I want to hide. And once again I come to an impasse.

"Cav's just got his panties in a bunch because he's all alone and destined to stay that way, only his hand for company."

There are snickers all round. But for once, Thomas isn't wrong. And yes, I know it's my own fault and doing but... is it so wrong to stay in whatever grace I have with my parents?

There's movement in my line of sight as Chloe walks past. She catches my eyes and detours over to me.

"What's up, pigs?" she asks while raising an eyebrow to me, silently asking if I'm okay.

I give her a small shrug.

She nods.

The guys are all tripping over being near her after

Chloe was seen with Sienna Star, LA's latest it girl, over the weekend.

"Oh, nothing," Thomas says, a smirk on his face. "We were just discussing how Cav here is going to end up old and alone."

"Is that so?" she asks.

He shrugs. "If your friends can't tell you the truth, who can?"

She nods. "But with friends like you, who needs enemies, huh?"

There's another chorus of "oooohs."

"So tell me, why are you destined to be alone?"

I shrug as Thomas answers. "Look at him."

"Oh, I'm looking," she purrs, moving closer to me.

I move my arm behind her legs, running my hand up her smooth thigh.

"Looks like he's not so alone right now."

Several mouths open while Thomas's jaw clenches.

"B-b-b-but…," Dan stammers.

"Yes?" Chloe asks, leaning on my shoulder.

"A-Aren't y-you, you know, w-with Sienna Star?"

"I'm sure she wouldn't mind having Cav be the meat in our sandwich. And just between you and me? He's the *only* one I'd consider as well."

I swear the guys about die.

She bends down, giving me and everyone else a good shot of her tits. "What do ya say, Cav?"

I give her my best panty-dropping smirk and hold my hand out to her. "I say we get out of here and take this party somewhere more private."

She puts her hand in mine.

"Have fun, fellas," Chloe says as we walk out.

"You okay?" she asks once we're out of the cafeteria.

"Not really."

"Thomas still being an ass?"

"When did he ever stop?"

"True."

"He's getting worse," she says.

I shrug.

"Connor says—"

I grab her arm. "What does Connor say?"

She blows out a breath. "That he's stubbornly sticking to his guns, and refuses to listen to anything Connor has to say. Jase is close to losing his shit and Amy's no help either. He's a bit stressed out about it. I think...."

"You think what?" I ask.

"I think that's why he's been so hesitant to end things with him. He doesn't want him to snap and say or do something, you know, *stupid*. He's a vindictive motherfucker. I think I'm right in saying none of us want to unleash that."

I run my hand over my head. "Fuck."

She shrugs. "Yeah. So what are you going to do about him?" Chloe asks.

"Not sure there's anything I can do about him. At least, not without him outing me."

"Have you even spoken to your parents lately?"

I shake my head. "I'm just...."

"Not ready to sever that connection completely," Chloe finishes for me.

"Am I mad?" I ask.

"No. But," she continues. "You *are* going to have to tell

them at some point. You can't—and shouldn't have to—hide who you are for the rest of your life."

"I know."

"And you know Thomas isn't going to stop either, right? He could even get worse. Do you want to leave Connor vulnerable and in his crosshairs?"

I sigh. "Of course I don't."

"So again, what are you going to do about it?" she asks, hands on her hips.

"That I *don't* know."

Her phone beeps, and she pulls it out. She smiles at whatever's on the screen, then looks to me. She looks to the screen again, then back to me.

"What?" I ask.

"I might have an idea, if you're interested? It's not a permanent solution, but it could get him off your back for a little while, at least."

"What've you got?" I ask.

"Well, it's no secret Thomas is a pig—"

"No, it's really not," I interrupt.

"And it's also no secret that he's been dying to have me. There have been more than a few times in the past where...." She trails off and her eyes become glassy. She shakes her head. "Anyway, he's trying to make you jealous with Connor. Why don't we turn the tables on him? Sienna's still in town and...."

"You're suggesting we have a *threesome*?" I almost screech.

She shrugs.

"Why not? Sienna would be down for it."

I laugh. "That's.... That's...."

"Look, I'm not saying we actually have to do anything. Just a few pics, maybe a quick video. We'll send it to a few people, who will send it to a few, who send it to a few more and so on and so forth. It won't cure you of all your Thomas ails, but it'll shut him up for a while, give you some breathing space."

I nod. I know he will. This is too juicy a secret, and he has too much animosity to keep it to himself.

"So, what do you say?"

I chew on my lip for a bit.

"Seriously, Cav," Chloe says. "We won't do anything, just play it up for a bit." She takes a breath. "I know what it's like to hide and not be ready to come out. I also know what Connor means to you. Your idiot friends may not notice, but for everyone else with half a brain, it's pretty obvious."

I chuckle. "And here I was thinking I hid it pretty well."

"So what do you say?"

CHAPTER 17

Chloe calls Sienna and tells her to meet us at my penthouse. You'd think filming a threesome would be easy, but when you specifically have distribution in mind, a lot more goes into it. It's all, "put your hand here, don't move your head, there," then "touch me here, suck me there." Not that I'm doing any sucking. The touching is unavoidable.

"What do you think?" I ask, sitting back on my haunches as Chloe reviews what we've got.

"I think it's hot," Sienna says, looking over her shoulder.

"Is it believable?"

She looks up. "Oh, yeah."

"It's good stuff," Chloe adds. "Just enough that it looks like you're into it, but it doesn't go too far. Although I think we could add to that if we want."

"Huh?"

"Well, I was thinking, and people—"

"You mean Thomas," I interrupt.

She shrugs. "—might find it weird we stopped where we did. But if we 'accidentally' knocked the camera and all you can see is a black screen but *hear* the rest, it might quash those doubts."

"So what, we all moan as we knock the headboard into the wall?"

Chloe grins at me. "That's *exactly* what we do."

Fifteen minutes later, we've moaned up a storm and almost put a dent in my wall.

"You two fake orgasms very convincingly," I comment.

Chloe shrugs.

"When you've been with the number of losers I have been," Sienna says, "it becomes a necessary skill."

"And no one's been able to tell?"

"If they have, they haven't cared enough to do anything about it."

"That's fucked-up," I tell her.

It's her turn to shrug. "Guys just don't care. Or maybe I picked the wrong ones; I don't know."

"So are you, like, bi or…." I trail off.

"If I had to put a label on it, I'd say bi, but honestly, it's not a thing for me. I want who I want. I don't think about whether they're male or female."

I nod.

"What about you?" Chloe asks.

"I'm gay all the way," I say.

"Yeah?"

"Yeah. I've lost count of all the girls my parents have set me up with, but they just don't do it for me."

"Who was it for you?" Chloe asks.

"Zac Efron."

She nods.

"The pretty boys do it for ya, huh?" Sienna asks.

"I guess."

"Connor's a pretty boy…." Chloe says, tapping her chin and giving me a coy look.

"Connor's…. He's, um…."

"It's okay," she concedes. "We get it."

"Have you spoken to him recently?" I ask.

"A few texts here and there. He's doing okay."

"He's healing okay?"

She nods. "Yup, all good so far."

"Good."

"Have *you* spoken to him?"

"Once."

"And?" Chloe demands.

"And we talked, but it came down to the same shit it always does."

"Look, I don't know you, but even I can tell you two are a mess," Sienna says.

"It's complicated."

"Or are you making it that way?" she rebuts.

"Maybe."

"Do you want to be with him?" Chloe asks.

I shoot her a look. "You know I do, if I could."

"Couldn't you just, you know, keep it on the DL?" Sienna asks.

"Connor deserves more than being my dirty little secret. Plus, nothing with me is ever on the DL. Too many people interested in what I'm doing and who I'm doing it with."

"Are you sure your parents would be that against it?"

I laugh. "You do know who my mom is, right?"

"A senator?"

I nod. "Senator and darling of the ultra-conservative right. To say she thinks homosexuals are an abomination is putting it lightly."

"You're going to have to do it at some point," Chloe says with a sigh.

"I know."

"And not to be a dick, but what are you waiting for? They've already all but disowned you. What more can they do?"

It's a good question, and the answer is "not much," but still....

She rolls over to face me. "You know what you need to do."

I rub my hands over my face.

She grabs my hand and pulls it away. "I know it's all kinds of terrifying, but seriously, Cav, you can't live like this. And neither can Connor."

Hours later, I'm still lying in bed, the faint scent of Chloe and Sienna's perfumes surrounding me—it's not altogether unbearable—when my phone rings.

"A threesome?" Connor says when I answer.

I shrug. "It sounded like a good idea at the time."

"I'm sure it did." I can hear the smile in his voice.

"And I was in no way into it," I add for reasons that escape me.

"I didn't think you would be."

"It's just Thomas…. I-I had to do something."

"Has he done something?"

"No. Well, not past what he's already threatened to do."

"I'm sorry."

"It's not your fault."

"Isn't it?" he asks.

"No, it's not." I blow out a breath. "It's me he's going after. I should have to live with the consequences."

"Fuck that, you shouldn't have to put up with anything."

"That's a nice idea, but it's not what happens in real life."

"Why can't it be?"

"Because good things don't happen to bad guys like me."

"You're not a bad guy, Cav."

"No?" I laugh.

"No, you're not." He leaves no room for arguing. "I'll end things with him. Today. Tonight. Right now. I'll get him out of the house, call the cops if I have to. I should never have let it go on this long in the first place. I fucking hate that you're feeling like you don't deserve anything good. You do, Cav, you deserve all the good things. So I'll end it. If you're ready…."

My heart soars at his words. "Yeah, I think I am. I want to talk to my parents," I tell him. "T-To tell them. About me." My conversation with Chloe and Sienna this afternoon reinforced just how messed up my situation is, and how it really is unfair to me and to Connor to live like this. Besides, I want to be with him. I *have* to be with him.

"Do you want me to come?" he asks.

"No. No way. There's no way I want you anywhere near the ugliness that's sure to ensue."

"I don't care about any of that," he tells me.

"I know you don't and I-I, I mean, I'm grateful for it, but I think I need to do this on my own."

"The offer's there."

"Thanks."

"So we're really doing this?" he asks.

"If you want."

"Oh, I want. I majorly want."

I laugh. "Yeah, me too."

CHAPTER 18

With a shaking hand, I tap the number on my screen and call.

It rings a few times before he picks up.

"Hello?"

"Hi, Dad, it's um, me, Cav."

"Yes, Cavanaugh?"

"I was, um, wondering if I could come over and talk to you and the senator about something?"

"If you're looking to overturn our divorce arrangement, I'm afraid that's not possible."

"No, that's not it. I'm um, fine with the arrangement."

"Good."

"So, can I come over?" I ask.

"The senator's in Washington at the moment."

"Oh, I didn't think the Senate was in session right now." In fact, I checked it wasn't.

"It's not, but she was needed on the Hill for some meetings."

"Any idea when she'll be back?"

"A couple of weeks or so, she said."

My heart sinks.

"Oh. Okay."

"If you'd like, you can make an appointment for when she's back."

An appointment. A fucking appointment like I'm just another inconsequential meeting on her busy, busy schedule.

"Sure. I'll call Aiden and organize something."

"That would be best. Goodbye."

He ends the call before I can say anything else.

Holy fuck. I run my hands over my face. I know I put this off for so long, but now I just want it over with. At least Connor will be back at school, so that's one thing to look forward to.

Speaking of….

"Hey," I say, answering his call. I know we only just spoke but I don't care. Any chance I get to hear his voice, I'm going to take. Although I have to wonder what's so urgent that he has to call again so soon.

"How'd it go?" he asks.

"About as well as I thought. The Senator's in DC, so I have to make an appointment for when she's back."

"Seriously?"

"Mmm."

"Holy shit."

"Eh. How are things over there?"

"Yeah, not good."

I bolt up. "What?"

"I mean, what did we expect? He was never going to go easily."

"Is he.... Are you.... Do you.... What can I do?" I finally settle on.

"I think I've convinced him to leave, but I'm going to give him some space to clear out. Jase said he'll stay and make sure he leaves, so I'm just walking to the L."

"Are you okay to do that? And is Jase okay being left alone with him?"

He chuckles, and it goes straight to my stomach. And lower. "I'm fine and so will Jase. Thomas's problem is with me, not my brother. But thank you for caring."

I blow out a breath. "If you say so." There's a pause before I break it. "So, you've been given clearance to go back to school?" I ask.

"Yup. The doctor said I'm healing nicely but not to push myself too much."

"So no blowjobs in the bathroom then?" Shit, why did I say that? Now I'm hard.

"Oh, baby, as much as I'd love to, I think that's going to have to wait. Hopefully not long, though."

I'm silent. He called me baby. I know he said it when we were together at the party, and I know I said it to him when he was in the hospital, but this time it's for keeps.

"Cav?" he asks. "Are you still there?"

"Y-y—" I clear my throat. "Yeah."

"What happened? What's wrong? Where'd you go?"

"Nothing, it's all good."

"Something happened."

"You called me baby," I whisper.

"Oh."

"I liked it," I tell him. "A lot."

"Did you now?" I can tell he's smirking.

"Switch to FaceTime," I order.

"Bossy, bossy," he says, but a second later his beautiful face pops up on my screen.

"There you are." I smile.

"Here *we* are."

"We. I like that."

"Me too," he says.

"You want to know how much I like it?" I ask.

He looks around and leans against the side of a building. "Show me."

I switch the camera so he gets a good look at my erection straining against my sweats.

He groans.

"That might just be the meanest thing you've ever done to me," he says.

"Oh, baby, I haven't even started yet," I tell him.

It's his turn to be silent. At least I can see his face this time.

I raise an eyebrow.

"Tell me the truth," he says. "When I was in the hospital, you called me that, didn't you?"

"What do you think?" I counter.

"I think you did. I think you stayed with me as long as you could and probably even used your name to make sure I got the best care."

"You would've done the same."

He nods.

"About that night—"

"You don't have to say anything."

"No, I do." I take a breath. "I'm so fucking sorry. I saw you and Thomas, and I got all in my head and it was… it was too much for me. I never thought you'd follow me, and I never, ever thought what happened would happen. I-I never want anything bad to happen to you."

"I know."

"It kills me to think what I did to you."

"What you did…. Cav, *you* didn't do anything. It was my choice to follow you. My decision to drive like a maniac when I knew the roads weren't closed. What happened was all me."

I'm shaking my head.

"No, listen, and really listen, please. You were *not* the cause of the accident, okay? That was *all* me, and I will go to my grave saying that."

"You were following me," I say. "And don't mention going to your grave."

He chuckles. "I won't mention going to my grave if you agree that you didn't cause the accident."

"You were following me," I repeat.

"Babe, I'd follow you anywhere."

My breath leaves me, while on the screen, his eyes go soft and he gives a smile.

"Are we agreed?" he asks.

I open my mouth.

"Unless the next word out of your mouth is 'okay,' I don't want to hear it."

I stare him down, but the jackass stares back.

"Don't test me, babe," he says.

"How about you not test me?" I counter.

"You started it."

"How old are you? Six?"

He raises an eyebrow.

"All right, all right," I relent.

"All right, what?" he asks.

"All right, I won't mention me being the cause of the accident," I say. But I'll still think it, no matter what he says or does to convince me.

He nods. "Good. I know I can't control what goes on in your pretty little head, but I don't want you thinking it, either."

"Pretty?" I scrunch up my nose. "There's nothing pretty *or* little about me." I switch cameras and give myself a squeeze over my sweats.

"Stop doing that," he groans.

"Why? You want it?"

"You know I do."

"How badly?"

"*So* fucking badly."

I switch the camera back to me. "Just remember that next time you think you can boss me around."

"You're a dick."

"You love it." Oh, fuck. I did *not* mean to say that. "I mean...."

Connor raises an eyebrow. "I'm telling you now, I won't be the first to say that."

"What?"

"When we get there, and we *will* get there, I'm telling you I won't be the first one to say it. I want you to break down and commit to me one hundred percent, so *you're* going to be the first one to say it."

"I'm already committed to you one hundred percent," I say, the words out of my mouth before I realize what I'm saying.

"In private you are." He holds up a hand when I go to retort. "And I know you're working on publicly, but only once that's done, will you be all mine."

I moan. "I like the sound of that."

"What?"

"Being all yours."

"Me too, baby, me too."

"So you're getting on the L?" I ask.

He nods. "Yeah. I thought it was best to give him some space. Plus, I *really* don't want to be around him anymore."

"Where are you headed now?"

He shrugs.

"Come to me," I tell him.

He gives me a look.

"Seriously, come here. We can hang out until everything dies down, then I'll take you home. Or you know, you could stay."

He shakes his head.

"I'll even pick you up at the station so you don't have to walk that far. I still think you shouldn't be walking that much by the way."

He rolls his eyes. "I'm not an invalid."

I arch an eyebrow. "You were in a bad accident and had major surgery, you should not be pushing yourself."

He growls.

"Any news on your car?" I ask, changing the subject.

"The insurance paid out, but Amy's punishing me and not letting me have the money. She took my ATM card."

"Dude, you really are in junior high."

He sighs. "I know, right?"

"I could—"

"Don't even think about it."

"Why not?" I ask as I pull out into the relatively light Chicago traffic.

"Because this is between me and Amy."

"You know she's going to get you a Hyundai or something."

"She can do that. But once I graduate, my money's mine. There's nothing she can do about that."

I shake my head. "We're gonna be two cashed-up idiots terrorizing the streets of Chicago."

He chuckles. "Sound good to me."

I nod. "Me too, baby."

When I finally get to the station, I find Connor sitting on the side of the road.

"I thought I said I'd pick you up," I say when I get out to help him in.

"And I thought I told you I'm not an invalid." He smacks my hand away.

"Until you get a clean bill of health from your doctors in a few weeks, I'm going to treat you like one."

"How do you know when I'll get a clean bill of health?" he asks.

"I, er, may have, um, done some, um, research," I say, scratching the back of my neck.

He chuckles and quickly squeezes my arm. "You really are cute, you know that?"

"Whatever." My cheeks heat.

He laughs. "Come on, help me into this beast of a car."

I help him in, and zip through the Chicago traffic to my building.

· · ·

"Wait a minute, and let me help you out," I tell him once I've parked.

He rolls his eyes but does as he's told.

"Good boy," I tell him, as I help him out.

He presses his body tight against mine. "You can be incredibly sweet, you know that?" he asks as he grabs onto my hips.

He smells like clean sheets, vetiver, and mine.

"I have my moments."

He chuckles as I lean down and brush my lips against his.

He moans and deepens the kiss, his tongue demanding entrance to my mouth, which is willingly given.

He tastes exactly like what I told him I thought he would, all those months ago when we were just random guys on Poundr.

Eventually the need for oxygen necessitates the breaking of the kiss, but I leave my forehead leaning on his.

"Hi," I say.

"Hi, back."

"You shouldn't have done all this," I tell him.

"I couldn't stay in the house. There was no way Thomas would've left if I'd stayed. Would you rather me sit in some diner on the south side?"

"Fuck no." I bring him closer to me. "You belong with me."

He chuckles. "There you go again, being all sweet."

This time it's him who brings his lips to mine. I love the feel of his lips against mine. Firm. Warm. Strong. I run my hands over his shoulders, down his arms, across his back. He's so solid underneath my palms. To think I could've lost this, or never had it at all.

"Mmm," he says as we break apart.

I give him one more chaste kiss. I can't get enough, won't ever get enough.

"Thanks for coming to get me," he whispers, his head now resting on my chest.

"You're welcome, baby."

He reaches around and gives my ass a squeeze.

"What was that for?" I ask.

He looks up at me. "You called me baby. To my face. While I'm conscious and not over a phone."

I chuckle.

"I liked it. A lot."

I kiss his neck. "Good, 'cause you're gonna be hearing it a lot."

"Yeah?"

I nod. "Yeah."

He nuzzles my neck, and I run my hand through his hair.

"Mmmm, that feels good," he moans, my dick jerking in my sweats.

He smothers a yawn, and I know I need to get him upstairs.

"Come on," I say, reluctantly, *very* reluctantly pulling away from him. "Let's go up."

"So, how have you been?" I ask as we stand in the elevator, him pressed closely to my side.

"Okay. Recovery hasn't been fun, especially with a concussion, but I'm getting there."

"And Thomas?"

"Besides the fact that he was there all. The. Time? For the most part he's been great, I suspect in large part due to how much he knew it would bug you. It got a bit… dicey in parts, but it's over now and in the past."

"I suppose I could be the bigger man and say as long as you were being looked after but…."

"But it really did piss you off."

"Yeah. The bit where it wasn't me, not that you got good care." The elevator dings and we exit into my penthouse. I guide him over to the couch.

He slings my arm around his shoulders and threads his fingers through mine. "I know, babe."

A warmth goes through my chest at the endearment. I rub the back of his hand with my thumb.

"How'd Thomas react when you told him to get out?" I ask.

"Leave *and* breaking up with him," he corrects. "And he took it as well as you'd expect."

"So not at all well."

He nods. "Pretty much. I'm not going to lie, I am concerned about what he's going to do next, but staying with him for that reason really wasn't a good enough excuse."

I nod. "It'll be fine." I'm not going to lie, I am concerned about what Thomas will do next, but I feel a shit ton better knowing Connor's not with him anymore.

"I hope so. He's… well, he's not happy."

"I wouldn't expect him to be. If I lost you… well, to say I'd be upset is putting it mildly."

"Aww, babe," he says, pulling my arm around him

tighter. "Are you worried about him?" he asks. "About him saying stuff?"

I shrug. "Not really. I've made an appointment to talk to my parents, so there's that. Besides, they've already kicked me out and legally disowned me. What else can they do?"

He rubs the base of my neck with his other hand.

"I'm sorry."

"It is what it is. Really, I'm probably better off. At least this way I'm not under their thumb and there's nothing they can hold over me." I turn to face him briefly. "At least I can be with you."

"In that case, I'm not sorry."

I chuckle.

"So, soon enough we'll be free of both Thomas and your parents. What will we do next?"

"Live happily ever after?" I suggest.

"What does that look like to you?" he asks, still massaging my neck.

I blow out a breath. "I don't even know. I've spent my whole life hiding who I am but having everything planned out for me. It's weird to realize that's not my path anymore."

"Feels good though, right?"

I sneak another quick peek at him. "Feel fantastic."

"So, um, what does the future look like to you?" I ask.

"Ah, I guess I hadn't really thought that far either." He chuckles.

"Do you want to go to college?" I ask.

As a McLaughlin, I have legacies at both Northwestern

and Yale. It was strongly suggested that I move to Connecticut.

"I don't know, maybe? I don't know what I'd want to major in, but I'm sure my parents would've wanted to me to go."

"We've got time, right?" I ask.

"Not really. Deadlines for applications will come up fast."

"Yeah, I guess."

He squeezes my hand again. "But we don't have to think about it if you don't want to."

"But we probably should."

"Probably."

"You know, I thought being free of all my parents' bullshit would lead to *less* decisions, not more."

He kisses the back of my hand. "Sorry, babe."

"As long as I'm doing it with you, I don't care."

"I don't either."

CHAPTER 20

For a while we sit in silence, both of us lost in our own thoughts.

"What now?" I ask eventually, breaking the silence.

"What do you mean?"

"I mean, are we boyfriends, not boyfriends, enemies?"

"I guess that depends on you," he says.

"Do you think it'll be too soon if you move from Thomas to me? You know, will people judge you for that at school?"

"Maybe. Probably. I don't really care though."

"Do you think people will believe us? That we're legit?" I ask. "I mean, everyone thinks I tried to kill you. Now all of a sudden I'm gay and we're together." It still feels weird to say that, but in a good way.

"Is this you having regrets?" He pulls his hand out of mine.

I grab it and hold it tight. "I will *never* regret you or us, I'm just thinking about... logistics."

He shakes his head.

"Plus, Chloe was going to leak the threesome video today."

He throws his head back and groans.

"Sorry."

"Hey." His eyes snap to mine. "Enough with the apologizing. You have nothing to be sorry for. This is all because of Thomas. If I hadn't tried to get back at you through him, this wouldn't be happening."

"He wouldn't have come to you if he wasn't trying to get at me," I remind him.

"I used him as much as he used me," he says.

"Whatever. It's done now, so let's try to move on."

He kisses the back of my hand again. Words can't describe how much I love it. "We'll play things as they come?"

I blow out a breath. "Yeah, okay."

His phone beeps and a text from Jase pops up.

Jase: Coast is all clear. Almost had to call the cops, but eventually he left and didn't totally wreck the place.

"I suppose I should get you home, huh?" I ask, even though that's the last place I want him to be. I want him to stay here, with me, for the rest of time.

He sighs. "I suppose."

The drive to Amy's brownstone is quiet, but not uncomfortable. Every moment that I can, I hold Connor's hand. While it's not everything I want, it's enough. For now.

. . .

W hen we get to the house, I order him to stay put again and rush around to help him out.

He rolls his eyes but smiles. "So this is how it's going to be, huh? You being all domineering and sexy and shit?"

I scratch the back of my neck. "I, ah, don't know about being, um, sexy, but I'll always want to do things for you and make sure you're okay. If that makes me domineering, then it is what it is," I say as we walk up the steps.

He unlocks the door and lets us in before pushing me up against the wall. "And that, babe, is sexy as fuck." He takes my lips in a blistering kiss.

I pull him to me, our bodies pressed so tight you couldn't even slip a piece of paper between us.

I will never tire of this. The feel of his lips against mine, the feel of his body pressed so close to mine we could almost meld together. Connor was right when he said we'd get to the love part, I just don't know if he knew it would be less than two hours after he initially said it.

"Oh, gross," Jase says, popping our bubble. "I did *not* need to see that."

Connor slips his arm around my waist and pulls me to his side. "It's nothing you haven't seen before," he hits back.

Jase shrugs. "That's true. C'mon, Amy's waiting for you."

Connor groans, then grabs my hand, pulling me further into the house.

· · ·

I f Amy's surprised to see me, she doesn't show it.

"Mr. McLaughlin, it's nice to see you again," she says.

"Er, you too," I say at the same time as Connor asks, "Is it?"

She stares at her brother. "Of course it is. Don't you know who his mother is?"

"A homophobic sycophant hell-bent on ridding the world of all who disagree with her?" he asks.

I smother my laughter.

"Connor!" Amy scolds.

"He's not wrong, Miss Siddell," I tell her. "You don't need to suck up to me because of her position. I neither care about it, nor will it get you anywhere or anything."

"She's a United States Senator."

"That doesn't mean she's a good person."

"Leave him alone, Aims. I'm relatively certain Cav knows his mom better than you do," Connor says.

She glares at him again.

"So you two are a thing, then?" she asks.

Connor grabs my hand and squeezes. "Yeah, we are. Is that a problem?"

She sighs. "As long as you promise that there will be no more street racing."

I wince. "I can absolutely guarantee that," I say.

Connor's head whips to me. "Are you serious?"

"If it means you don't get hurt again, absolutely."

He growls.

"Don't press me on this, babe," I warn.

"I think you should listen to your boyfriend," Amy tells

me. "I don't think you want to end up in the hospital again, do you?"

"It's not like I planned it," he says. "Or wanted it to happen. If I had my choice, I would've driven off into the night and come back to collect Cav's car the next day." He shoots me a wink.

I scoff. "In your dreams." We never did find out who won the race, not that it matters or either of us cares.

"Oh, baby, you have no idea the kind of things I dream about." The gleam in his eye tells me he'd be more than happy for me to find out, though.

Amy shakes her head. "Seriously, Connor?"

"What? I can't flirt with my boyfriend?"

The word hits me in the chest. I know Amy said it before, but it's different when it comes out of Connor's mouth. Obviously between now and our conversation in my apartment, he's taken the decision out of my hands. To be honest, I thought I'd freak out hearing that, but I kinda like it. Actually, I kind of *love* it.

He turns to me. "I know I said labeling us would be up to you, but I want you to know I consider you my boyfriend and I'm okay with keeping that on the DL while you, um, sort things out."

All I can do is nod.

He squeezes my hand and turns back to his sister. "And contrary to your opinion, Aims, I didn't have my accident on purpose, and we *were* in a good place. Yes, I fucked that up, but it was the first time in weeks I'd put a foot wrong. I'm young, I'm dumb, I'm a guy. I'm going to fuck up, but it's not a personal affront to you, it's just what I do."

I shift my weight from foot to foot. I really don't think I should be here for this conversation, but Connor still has hold of my hand and won't let go. "Um, this seems like a private thing, so maybe I should, ah, go?" I don't mean to phrase it as a question, but that's how it comes out.

"You're not going anywhere," Connor grits out.

"Babe, this is between you and your sister. Work it out in private."

His eyes soften at the endearment. "Fine, but wait in my room, would you please?"

I give him a smile and a chaste kiss. "Sure."

Connor's room is your typical teenage boy's room. Dark colors, minimal decoration. I flop onto his bed and am immediately enveloped by my favorite smell in the world: Connor.

"So you and Connor are official now?" Jase asks, standing at the door to Connor's room.

"Not out official, but we're together, yeah," I reply, sitting up.

"And this…. You two…. It's for real? You're not playing him or using him?"

I want to tell him coming out to my parents will incur their wrath, something that's not lightly done, but I realize he's just looking out for his brother.

"It's for real," I say. "If he wants me, it'll be forever."

Jase's eyes go wide, his jaw dropping slightly.

I take a breath. "I know Connor's and my relationship didn't get off to the most conventional of starts—"

He snorts.

"—but," I continue. "I love him and I want to be with him as long as he'll have me."

Jase nods. "Okay."

"Okay?"

"Yeah, okay."

"What? No lecture? No threats? No ten-minute monologue on how I'm such a horrible person and in no way deserve to be with such an awesome guy like your brother?"

"I figure that goes without saying."

I nod.

He continues. "I trust my brother, and I love him to death. He was my rock when we were in Michigan. There wasn't anything he wouldn't do for me. He's a good guy, Cav. The best. And I want to see him happy. He deserves it. So if you make him happy, then I'm happy. I'm not going to stand here and say I know what's best for him. I'm fifteen, what would I know? My brother's also smart enough to know that if a relationship isn't working, he needs to get out, and he does. Quickly. So no, I'm not going to lecture or threaten. But I am going to ask that you not hurt him and warn you that if I see something, *anything* I don't like, I won't hesitate to do something."

I nod. "I can do that. The, uh, accident notwithstanding."

"Connor said it wasn't your fault, so it's not."

"Doesn't mean I don't feel horrible about it."

"I know."

"Thanks, Jase. I know we were sorta friends before, but I'd really like it if we could continue that?"

He gives me a small smile. "Apparently you're going to

be around forever, so I guess that would probably be a good idea."

I cringe a little. "Yeah, look. I'm not freaking out about what that means or entails, but if you could not tell Connor I said that, that would be great."

He chuckles. "Don't want to be the first one to say it, huh?"

"According to Connor, I will be the first. I just… don't want to say it just yet."

He nods. "Treat 'em mean, keep 'em keen."

I laugh. "Something like that."

"Just don't keep him too keen. He deserves good things."

"Just to be clear, I'm a good thing, right?"

He rolls his eyes. "Yeah, Cav, you're a good thing. Just keep it that way."

CHAPTER 21

Connor comes up a little while later, sitting on the bed next to me. I chuckle, rolling over to my side and rubbing his chest.

"Everything okay?" I ask.

He blows out a breath. "Yeah, I guess so. It's just hard, having basically been the parent while Mom and Dad were sick, to be here and Amy trying to fill that role."

"I'm sure she means well."

He picks up my hand and kisses it before holding it to his chest. "I'm sure that's exactly why she's doing it, but it's too little, too late. I'm eighteen, an adult. I can look after myself, have been looking after myself as well as Jase for years. But now Mom and Dad are gone, and all of a sudden a piece of paper says I'm in Amy's care and she has control of my trust fund until I graduate. It's just… weird."

"At least she cares," I tell him. "And she's trying."

"Oh shit, babe, I'm sorry." He gingerly rolls to face me.

"It's fine. I'm better off without them, not that I ever really *had* them to begin with."

"Well, you have me," he says, pulling me close.

"Mmm." I nuzzle into his neck. "I can live with that."

He runs his hand through my hair, scratching my scalp.

"That feels *so* good," I all but purr.

"Did you ever think when you swiped on me, that we'd end up here?" he asks.

"Mmm, nope. I was kind of terrified of this, actually."

"But yet, here we are."

"Here we are. Trust you to force your way into something." I smile.

"Pfft," he scoffs. "You're *glad* I forced my way in."

I snuggle closer to him and brush my lips against his. "Yeah, I really am."

"Are you nervous about the meeting with your parents?"

"You mean the senator and her husband?" I correct. "Yes, and no. Yes, because they're still my parents and I know they're going to spew all sorts of hateful bullshit, but no, because they haven't been my parents in a long, long time. How'd your parents take it?"

"Fine. My dad was already terminal by then, so there was a lot of 'life's too short' kind of thing, but I like to think even if he had been healthy, they would've supported and accepted me."

"I'm sure they would have."

"How do you know?"

"Because hateful parents raise hateful kids. You're not hateful. Jase is about as far from hateful as you can get."

"I don't know about that. He's protective as hell. Plus, there were some times growing up when I would take one of his toys or something and he went off." He chuckles.

"Nah, he's a good kid," I argue.

"What about me?" he asks. "Am I a good boy?"

"You're the best," I tell him.

He chuckles again. "Aww, thanks, babe. Right back atcha."

"I think we both know I'm not a good guy."

He pulls back slightly. "Why? Because you can be an asshole?"

I give him a look. "I think we both know I can be more than an asshole."

"A bastard then."

"More than that too." I sigh. "I'm not a good guy, Connor."

He struggles to sit up. "That's bullshit. A bad guy wouldn't have looked out for me like you have after my accident. He wouldn't care for me like you care. You want to know what I think?" he asks. "I think you're a good guy who's been told he's a bad guy because it isn't who people need, want, or expect him to be."

I laugh. "Seriously?"

"Tell me why you think I'm wrong."

"I...." I start, then stop. The truth is, Connor might have a point, but I still think it's an incredibly simplistic and idealistic way of thinking about things.

"You can't think of anything, can you?" he says, the corner of his mouth ticking up.

"I've done bad things," I tell him. "Some really fucked-up things. A good person wouldn't do that."

"You're made mistakes; who hasn't?"

I shake my head. Calling what I've done mistakes makes it too easy to ignore them or explain them away. "Oh, that was a mistake, I didn't mean it," and poof! They disappear.

"Sometimes there aren't excuses for the things we do, Connor."

"Like what?" he asks.

I shake my head. "Just stuff. Stuff that I'm not proud of."

"There," he says, grabbing my hand.

"Where?"

"Where you said, and I quote, 'stuff that I'm not proud of.' If you *were* truly a bad guy, you wouldn't give a fuck about the things you've done and you definitely wouldn't feel bad about them."

"Why are you pushing this so hard?" I ask.

"Why are you *fighting* this so hard?" he counters.

"Because I don't want you going into this with your eyes closed."

He gets up on his knees and walks over to me, straddling my lap and cupping my face. "Baby, there is nothing you can say or do to me that will have me turning away from you, okay?" He looks deep in my eyes. "I know this is a huge thing for you and you're probably scared and worried, even if you don't want to admit it, but I'm here with you. Every step of the way. We all have our pasts. Good, bad, or indifferent, they shape who we are today. I'm not with you because of a joke or because you're great in bed and make me come like a freight train, okay? I'm with you because of this." He brushes my forehead. "And because of this." He lays his hand on my chest, over my heart. "I know what I see in you, and nothing you can say or do can change that, do you hear me?"

Reluctantly, I nod.

"Good."

I chuckle and lift my hips where my dick is pushing against my sweats. "You're so fucking sexy when you're on a crusade."

He moans, resting his forehead on my shoulder as he grinds against me. "I want you so badly," he grits out.

I take hold of his hips. "I know, baby. Me too. But we can't. You're still healing, and I don't want to do anything that may jeopardize that."

He groans and slips off me. "See? That right there is something a good guy would do."

I look at the bulge in his jeans.

"Bet you're wishing I wasn't right now, aren't you?"

He adjusts himself, wincing slightly. "Yeah, just a bit."

I laugh and fit myself to his side again. "But we can still make out, right?"

He rolls to face me. "Why yes, yes we can."

CHAPTER 22

The next day when I pull up to school, my lips are still bruised from Connor and my epic make-out session yesterday.

I smile at the memory. Being with him is…. Well, it's nothing short of bliss. He's who I want to be with, who I want to spend the rest of my life with. And maybe I sound like a chick admitting that, but I don't give a fuck.

Connor Siddell is everything I'm not. He makes me want to be, though. For him, there's nothing I won't do.

Including have a pretend threesome with his best friend and her… friend.

There are back slaps and congratulations galore as I walk down the hall to my locker.

"Holy shit, Cav, man," Dan says. "That tape…." He gives me a nod and a wink.

"Is it not the slightest bit weird for you to admit to your friend that you watched his sex tape?" I ask.

"I, er… yes?"

"Lord knows it's something you'll never experience yourself, but it's a little weird," I tell him.

Usually I'd accuse him of being more than a little gay, but I can't stomach the words coming out of my mouth. See? Progress is being made. Connor would be proud. And that right there keeps my mouth even more firmly shut.

"What was it like?" Pete asks, his eyes darting everywhere but me.

"It was terrible," I deadpan. "Worst experience of my life."

"Really?" he asks, eyes wide.

I smack him on the back of the head. "No, you idiot, it was incredible. I came so hard I couldn't feel my toes for an hour."

"Oh. Thought so." He nods. "But, ah, why Chloe?" he asks.

"You think I don't know how long Thomas has been lusting after her?" I ask. "We saw an opportunity to shove it to him, put him back in his place, so we took it."

"Oh. And um, Connor?"

"What about Connor? He's got nothing to do with this."

"Oh, I um, just thought, seeing as though she's his friend it might be…."

"Might be what?"

"You know, something else to get at him."

I sigh and close my locker. "Look, I know I went at Connor hard, but that's over now. It's done."

"And Thomas?" Dan asks.

"Thomas needs to remember his place," I tell them. "Something all of you would do well to remember."

"Yes, Cav," they mumble.

"I can have anyone I want, when I want, and I will take as I please. Got it?"

They nod.

"Any*one*?" Thomas asks, coming over to us. "Or any *girl*?"

"Is there a difference?" Dan asks.

"I don't know, Cav, is there?" Thomas raises an eyebrow.

I slap his face, not hard, but hard enough not to be friendly. "Look, I know you're all in your pansexual-ness, but we've had this conversation before. You're not my type, and I don't need to fuck you for you to be my bitch, you were born that way. But I am flattered by the attention."

"Aren't you with Connor?" Pete asks Thomas. "Why would you be flirting with Cav when you have a boyfriend?"

"Oh, didn't you hear?" Chloe says, coming up to us. She reaches up and kisses my cheek. I slip an arm around her waist. "Connor broke up with Thomas yesterday. He told me he had fun seeing how far he could push him, but in the end, he was such a bore, Connor just wasn't into it."

She giggles while Dan hides his snicker. Thomas's face is red, his fists clenched.

"Ah, that's um, too bad," Pete says.

Chloe shrugs. "What can I say? Sometimes you need a man."

I nod. "Don't feel too bad, Tom, man. I'm sure there's

someone out there who thinks you're man enough for him."

"And you think you're man enough?" he grits out.

I shrug. "Sure. Just ask this lovely lady and her stunning friend."

Chloe nods.

"He's probably *too* much man," she says, "but we managed to handle him. Just."

I shrug. "It's a curse."

"The curse of the big dick," Dan says.

"It's a tough life, but someone has to do it," I say.

Everyone but Thomas laughs.

I drop my arm and smack Chloe on the ass. "As much as I love seeing you, sweetheart, you should go find Connor. Wouldn't want him to have *too* much of a hard time his first day back, now would we?"

She gives a fake giggle and rises up to kiss me on the cheek again.

"You want another go, just give us a call," she says as she sashays away and throws in a wink for good measure.

"Ho-ly shiiiiiiiiiiiiiiiiiiiiiiiiiiiiiiiiit," Dan exclaims once she's out of sight. "You really *are* a god or something, aren't you?"

"I mean, I understand how it would appear that way, 'cause it's something that's never, *ever* going to happen for you. But for the rest of us…."

Again, everyone laughs.

"Nah, it wasn't really a big deal. We wanted to have some fun, so we did. End of story."

"And everyone that's seen the tape," Thomas adds.

"Seeing how it was mysteriously 'leaked.'" He makes air quotes. "Rather convenient, don't you think?"

"Convenient how?" I ask, leaning against my locker.

"You know. There're rumors going around about you and—"

"Rumors?" I ask. "What rumors?"

Pete shifts from foot to foot. "Just stupid stuff," he mumbles.

"Oh, you mean the stupid stuff that was coming out his mouth last week?" I throw a thumb in Thomas's direction. "Tell me, did anyone *actually* believe that?"

There's a chorus of "no" and a whole lot of shaking heads.

"So if no one believed it, and *I* certainly didn't believe it, why would I feel compelled to do this *and* release it?"

There are no answers.

I smack Thomas on the shoulder. "Good try, man, but it looks like once again you fall short. I would've thought you'd be used to it by now, but maybe you're just getting the hang of it."

His eyes flash. I give him a smile. He's not done with me yet, but I don't care. I have Connor, and soon I'll be able to have him in public. That's, *he's* all I care about.

CHAPTER 23

I'm heading to the cafeteria when a hand sneaks out of a closet and pulls me in. I start to struggle but stop when Connor's scent weaves its way into my senses.

"Shhh," he says.

"What the fuck are you doing?" I ask, my hands managing to find his hips in the darkness and pulling him to me.

He nuzzles my neck. "I was going crazy hearing about that stupid threesome you, Chloe, and Sienna had."

"*Pretended* to have," I correct.

"Whatever."

I chuckle as he nips and sucks at my neck and shoulder. "Jealous, are we?"

"Fuck yes, I am," he says.

"Oh, baby." I run my fingers through his hair.

"Three more weeks and hopefully I'll get the all clear from my doctors."

I groan and pull him tighter to me, our hardening

dicks rubbing against each other deliciously. "It'll be worth the wait," I say, a little breathlessly.

"Oh, I know it will be, but that doesn't mean I'm not horny as fuck now."

"I wish I could take care of that for you," I tell him. "But I don't want to hurt you or make you pull a stitch or something."

He leans over and kisses me. "I know you would, babe. Thank you, anyway."

"So tell me more about how you're jealous?"

He laughs and pushes me away. "Shut up."

"At least you know it's not real."

"This is true."

He sighs.

"I know." I press a kiss on his forehead. "You want to come over after school? We can hang out, grab deep dish, do whatever?"

"Mmm, okay."

"Hey." I direct his face to mine. "Are you okay?"

"I just… didn't think it'd be this hard to have to pretend that I hate you."

I smash my lips against his. Our tongues duel, teeth clash against the others, hands wandering everywhere. This guy…. *My* guy…. Eventually we break apart, panting.

"Soon," I promise.

"I know, and I'm fine with waiting. The finish line is in sight, it's just…."

"We've finally got our act together and you want to shout it from the rooftops?" I finish for him.

"Yeah."

I hug him to me tighter. No matter how close he is, it's never close enough.

"It's fine. I'm just being an idiot. They're weaning me off the pain meds so I'm a bit… whatever."

"And you're horny as fuck."

He chuckles. "That too."

"If I do all the work, do you think you'd be okay?" I ask, biting my lip.

"At this point, I'm willing to say 'fuck it' and just do it anyway."

I start undoing his slacks. "If at *any* time you're in pain, you *have* to tell me, okay?"

He nods. "Sure."

I drop his slacks but don't reach for his boxers. "I mean it, Connor. Even the slightest twinge or pull or anything, and you tell me straight away, okay?"

"I promise."

"Good boy." I press a kiss to his lips, then move down his body, kissing his still red but healed scars.

I pull down his boxer-briefs, his glorious dick almost hitting me in the face. Taking him in my mouth, I look up, never breaking eye contact with him.

"Oh, fuck, baby," he breathes as I take him deep.

"Okay?" I ask.

"It won't be if you stop doing what you were doing." He pushes my head toward his crotch again.

I chuckle and suck him deep before drawing back, sucking his crown and playing with his slit.

"Mmmm, Cav, baby, that feels so good," he moans. "I fucking love your mouth."

I smile, loving that I can do this to him, *for* him.

I work him over, his hands in my hair, but that's as far as I'll let him go. I'm terrified of hurting him, of setting his recovery back, but my man is hurting.

"Cav," he moans. "Babe, I'm about to come."

I moan around him and suck him deeper, harder. He spills down my throat, and I take every drop.

When he's spent, I lick him clean before pulling his boxers and slacks up and doing them up.

"How are you?" I ask.

His eyes are glazed over and slightly unfocused. "*So good.*"

"Are you hurting? In pain? Did you pull anything?"

He grabs the back of my head and pulls me to him, taking, owning my mouth.

"I'm fine, thank you," he says when we break apart.

I pull him to me, our arms slipping around each other's waists, his head resting on my shoulder.

"I don't want to go back out there," I tell him.

"Me either. Let's live in this closet for the rest of our lives."

I chuckle and kiss his forehead. I can't, won't ever, get enough of him. "A few more hours, then you'll come over. We can last."

"Maybe just a little longer now that you've sucked my brains out through my dick."

"You know all the right words to say to a guy, Mr. Siddell," I say in a high-pitched voice.

He laughs and hugs me to him tighter. "As long as you keep doing that, I'll flatter you all the time."

I kiss his forehead. "I can do that. But," I say with a sigh, "I should go."

He grips me tighter before nodding. "Yeah."

"I'll see you after school?"

"Wouldn't miss it for the world."

The first time I saw Connor Siddell in the parking lot of Windswept Academy, my heart leapt. Then immediately it sank to the floor. Yes, I knew he was going to be here, but something kept me from believing it. He couldn't be here. He couldn't. But fuck if it wasn't fate that he was.

And now we're here.

"This place is… nice," he says as we lie shirtless on my bed, my hand running up and down his back.

I chuckle. "Yeah, nice is one word for it."

"Are you okay with being here? You know, with everything your parents did and what it means?" He rubs my stomach, and my dick jerks in my sweats.

I shrug. "I didn't really have a choice, so it is what it is, I guess."

"Uh-huh," he murmurs, his lips brushing my cheek. "Anything else?"

"Is there supposed to be anything else?" I ask.

"You tell me, babe."

I hitch his leg over my hip, his other foot tangling with mine. "I don't know. I feel like… like this was kind of… I don't know… inevitable, I guess."

"How so?" He doesn't stop brushing his lips over my cheek or rubbing my stomach.

"I guess I just always felt like they were waiting until they could be rid of me. Now they've got their reason, and they took the opportunity and ran. Not that I can blame them."

"No matter what you've done, it's no excuse for how they treated you," he says.

I shrug. "Eh. It's not like they even wanted kids in the first place. I'm pretty sure the only reason they had me was because it was what was expected of them."

"I don't care if it's decreed by law that a married couple has to have children, that shouldn't be a reason to bring a person into the world."

"Mmm."

"That said, I am *very* glad they did have you."

I turn my head and kiss him quickly. "Thanks, babe."

"I just hate that you have such shit parents."

"Luck of the draw, I guess."

"What were your parents like?" I ask after a little while.

He smiles. "They were great. A little hopeless and more than a bit embarrassing, but looking back, I don't mind so much."

"How's that?"

"I knew fairly early in the game I wasn't like everyone else. While my friends were choosing girls to be 'married' to in the back of the school bus, I only had eyes for Henry Lazare, the new kid from New Orleans. As I grew, I realized I didn't like girls, and it had nothing to do with them having cooties."

I laugh.

"I came out to my parents in the middle of my dad's treatment. He was so sick but fighting hard to not look it. It was Thanksgiving, and he was going on about all the girls he thought would be clamoring for an invite to taste his famous sweet potato pie. I told him it wasn't the girls I was interested in, it was the guys. He just smiled and said, 'in that case, I better make two.'"

"T-That's great," I say through a thick throat.

"The next year he was too sick to do any baking and he, uh, died before the one after that."

I bring him tighter to me and kiss the top of his head. "I'm sorry."

He shrugs. "Cancer's a bitch."

I laugh. "Yeah, it is."

"What was your mom like?" I ask.

He smiles. "She was your typical suburban mom, except she was also the head of marketing for a local restaurant chain. She worked long hours but was at every PTA meeting, soccer game, and baked cookies for every bake sale. She, um, even tried to work through her treatments, but eventually she couldn't do it anymore. She never gave up, not even at the end. She was the reason I got into cars too. Her dad, my grandpa, worked for Chevy in Detroit. They used to fix up old cars together, then she did it with me."

"Wow."

He nods. "I want to be like them when I grow up."

"You want kids?" I ask after another pause.

"Sure. Two boys. Or a boy and a girl."

"Why not two boys and a girl?" I counter.

He laughs. "Okay, why not?"

"Adoption or a surrogate?"

"Adoption," he says quickly. "I want to give a home to someone, or someones who don't have one."

"Mmm, I like that."

He looks up at me. "I want to give those kids the kind of love you never had."

I swear to God my heart fucking stops. "Y-you w-want…."

"What do you say?" he asks. "Sound good to you?"

All I can do is nod. Truthfully, I've never thought of the future, of kids. I guess I always imagined my parents would win and I'd marry the daughter of one of their friends or whoever offered the most advantageous match. Eventually we'd have *a* kid, because again, that's what happens, and the cycle would repeat itself.

"What's it like to have siblings?" I ask, changing tack slightly.

"If you're asking about Amy, well… it's difficult. There's six years between us, but I feel like it's a lifetime, you know? There's three years between Jase and me, and it feels like nothing."

I nod. "How is Amy? Is she getting any better?"

He shrugs. "About the same. I get I screwed up, but I've apologized and learned from it. I feel like she'll never believe me, that she'll never trust me. It feels like we're always battling for something and neither of us know what it is, if it even exists anymore."

"And Jase?"

"Jase is protective of his family. Of me especially. I get it too. He lost both parents in horrific ways. For a long time, I was his only support. Then to have me get in a serious accident? I don't blame him for having PTSD when it comes to loved ones and hospitals."

"Shit, I didn't even think of that," I say.

"I think he's better now that I'm home and he can see for himself I'm okay and getting better, but I think that worry will always be there. He'll always be scared something may happen to me. I wouldn't want to cross him if he thinks I'm in danger."

"Well, you're not in danger."

He presses into my side. "No, I'm not." His lips find my neck and start to nip and suck.

"Mmm," I moan, my hand running through his hair.

"And before you ask, yes, I'm fine after today's… *activities* in the janitor's closet."

"That's good, so good, baby."

His hand wanders to the waistband of my now very tented sweats, running along the edge.

He chuckles. "But I feel bad that I didn't return the favor."

"It's fine," I breathe.

"Mmm, sorry, babe, that's not how a relationship works. I can't be the one who takes all the time. Neither can you, for that matter."

"So this *is* a relationship?"

He chuckles. "You just want me to call you my boyfriend again."

My dick jerks.

"You like that, huh?"

I nod.

"I'll have to remember that," he says as he slips his hand into my pants, taking me, stroking me, long and hard.

"Oh, fuck," I moan, my hips lifting to meet him.

"Have I told you how much I love your cock?" he asks. "So long, so hard, and it's all for me, isn't it?"

I nod. "Yes, yes."

"Good." He gives me another stroke, making sure he hits the sweet spot underneath.

"Connor," I moan.

"Yes, baby?"

"I want you."

"Oh, I want you too, but doctor's orders say not for a few weeks yet."

I force his head over to me, taking his lips with mine. He meets my tongue's strokes, the kiss going on for what could be hours.

"You drive me crazy," I say when we finally break apart.

"Right back atcha."

He's stroking me with vigor now, and I know it won't be long, the tingling coming in the base of my spine.

"I'm gonna come," I warn.

To my objection, he slips down the bed. "Wha—?" I ask, before he takes my tip in his mouth.

"Fuuuuuuuuuuuuuuuuuuuuuuuuuuuuuuuuuck," I exclaim,

coming long and hard, Connor staying with me through it all.

He wipes the corner of his mouth before tucking me away and crawling back up the bed.

"How was that?" he asks, sliding his arms around me.

All I can do is nod.

He chuckles. "Good."

It's a while before I come down enough to string a sentence together.

"Holy fuck," I breathe, running my hands over my face. I turn to him. "Thank you."

He kisses me. "You never have to thank me for that. I enjoyed it as much as you did."

I grab him by the back of his head and kiss him hungrily, tasting myself on his lips. "I'll thank you if I want to," I tell him.

He chuckles again, kissing me once more. "Okay then."

"So I guess this makes us official then," I say.

He smiles. "As official as you want it to be."

"I've made the appoint—"

"I know," he says, stopping me. "And I'm more than willing to go with you to said appointment if you want me to. But for now, we're exactly what you want us to be. I don't want to rush you or force you into doing anything you don't want, or aren't ready, to do."

I kiss him chastely. "You're the best, you know that?" In truth, I want to say something else to him, but I think I'll make him wait just a little bit longer. My bad boy habits die hard.

"I am well aware, yes," he says.

I roll my eyes but smile. "You're an ass."

"You can have it anytime you want, baby."

I pull back. "Really?"

"As soon as I get the all clear from the doc, I'm all yours."

I grip him tighter. "You're already mine," I say.

He nods. "Yeah, I am."

CHAPTER 25

Walking into school the next day, knowing Connor is mine and I'm his, everything feels… different. But good different. It's like… everything has fallen into place. All I need is to have my meeting with the senator and my dad once she's back from DC and I'll be free.

Free. Such a little word for a big fucking deal.

People stop and stare at me as I walked past with a smile on my face, but I don't care. I'm happy. For maybe the first time ever, I'm doing what *I* want. And soon I'll be free to be who I really am.

But my warm and fuzzy feelings are dampened when I see Connor and Thomas arguing. It takes everything I have not to go over there and punch Thomas in the face.

"You need to let it go," Connor says. "We're done."

"What if I'm not okay with that?" Thomas asks. "We had a deal, an agreement. You can't just go back on it. That's not how this works. It's not how it's supposed to go."

"I don't give a fuck," Connor replies. "It takes two to tango, and I'm not dancing any more."

Unable to stop myself, my feet carry me in their direction before I even realize what's happening.

"Lovers' tiff?" I ask.

Connor turns to face me and fuck, does he look good.

"Your boy here doesn't seem to understand what no means," he tells me, seamlessly slipping into our public roles.

I shrug. "He always was a little bit slow."

"Fuck off, Cav. You know you'd—" Thomas says before I cut him off. I don't know what he's going to say, but I'm willing to bet my penthouse it won't be good.

"You're pathetic," I tell him. "Man the fuck up, if you can."

"We're over, dude," Connor says. "I'd say it was fun, but was it?"

I snigger, and Thomas's head snaps to face me.

"Softening your stance, are we?" he asks.

I shrug. "You know what they say, the enemy of my enemy is my friend. Besides, I almost killed the dude, figured I owed him a favor or two."

"I'm your enemy?" Thomas asks.

"Are you my friend?" I counter. "How many times have you spread rumors to undermine me? How many times have you challenged me? You think that's being a friend?"

He stays silent.

"Yeah, that's what I thought," I say. "Do yourself a favor and get over the pretty boy here. You're embarrassing yourself, and begging is never a good look on anyone."

He clenches and unclenches his fists. "So that's how it is then, huh?"

I shrug. "I'm just picking up what you laid down."

He nods. "You think you're untouchable, don't you? The great Cavanaugh McLaughlin, safe with his mommy's senate seat protecting him. But what happens when you no longer have that protection, huh?"

"I'm fairly confident I can handle my own issues," I say. "But if running to *your* mommy and daddy makes you feel better...."

There's a smattering of laughs from the gathered crowd.

"Look," I say, putting on what I hope is a sympathetic face. "I don't know what happened between us, where we went wrong, but I'm sorry it did. Maybe it can be fixed, maybe it's damaged beyond repair, but I hope that as we figure it out, we can at least be civil." I pat him on the shoulder.

He shakes off my touch and laughs.

"This is how you're going to play it?" he asks.

"I'm not playing anything," I tell him, keeping my face blank. "I'm honestly trying to work through our issues, see if we can't get this friendship back on track. Isn't that what you want too?"

He shakes his head. "You're a piece of work, you know that?"

"But you've always known that. You've benefitted from it, hell, you've relished in it. I was the ass you didn't have the balls to be."

"You think you're so clever, don't you?" he asks.

I shrug. "When it comes to the two of us, I think we all know who will always come out on top."

"Yes, because the great Cavanaugh McLaughlin always wins, doesn't he?"

I take a step closer to him. "You lost," I tell him. "You tried to play the game and you lost, fair and square. Now why don't you do us all a favor and let it go." I pat his shoulder.

He knocks my hand away. "Don't fucking touch me."

I hold my hands up.

He turns to Connor. "Why is he so great, huh?" he asks. "He's an ass! He was horrible to you when you first got here, he's horrible to *everyone*! But no one will ever do anything! They all sit around and pretend to like him and wax poetic about how awesome he is and how they wish they could be like him. Why?! I don't get it!" He turns to gathered crowd. "Can somebody *please* tell me what is so fucking great about him? *Please?* Because I truly do not understand why you people let him get away with all the shit that he does."

Connor grabs the top of his arm. "Dude, I think you need to calm down."

"Calm down?" Thomas asks. "I need to calm down?! I don't want to fucking calm down! You guys have all been brainwashed, but I'm going to show you! I'm going to prove to you that he's not all that you think he is."

"Thomas—" Connor starts.

"No!" he says. "You had your chance. You threw it away and ruined everything! And for what? A loser like *him*?" He shakes his head. "Fuck you both," he says before walking off.

"Well, that was unexpected."

"Ah, yeah." I scratch the back of my head.

"What *was* that?" Connor asks.

"I have no idea. I've never seen Thomas that… whatever that was."

"Are you worried?"

"About him?"

"About what he might do," he corrects.

"Yes and no. Thomas talks a good game, but when push comes to shove, he never does anything. Besides, what kind of damage can he do?"

As it turns out, a lot.

CHAPTER 26

In the few weeks since Thomas's tantrum, I guess is the best word for it, the tide seems to have turned against him. And gives me an opportunity to be civil to Connor in public. In private, I'm very, *very* personal.

"So are you two, like, *buddies* now?" Dan asks as we all, Connor and Chloe included, sit in the cafeteria.

"You didn't buy the enemy of my enemy is my friend thing?" I ask.

"I mean, it makes sense," Pete says. "Especially how Thomas, you know, lost it that day. You two are like, teaming up to defeat evil."

"Defeat evil?" I chuckle.

"What are you on?" Connor asks. "And can I have some? Sharing is caring, man."

Pete blushes.

"Look," I say, putting down the lid of the orange Gatorade I was playing with. "It's pretty obvious Thomas didn't take Connor breaking up with him well." Not that I can blame him on that one. I'd be more than a wreck if it were ever to happen to me. "And I know things have been tense between the two of us, but that was all him. I don't know what his problem is, but it's that, *his* problem, not mine. Maybe it was all too much for him when Connor here saw the light and realized what a loser Thomas is. Maybe he didn't get enough hugs as a kid, I don't know. What I do know is that *no one* talks shit about me, threatens me, or tries to harm me. Connor is obviously a weak spot for him, so if he's of help to me, then so be it." I turn to Connor. "I hope you don't mind me putting it in those terms." Stepping back into the bad boy role feels... strange, but also familiar. Being with Connor, it's like I can almost forget that's who I was, who I am. One thing is for certain though, it's not who I want to be.

He shakes his head. "No problem here. In fact, I was going to say the same thing. Thomas is crazy. He was using me to get at Cav and when that didn't work he threw a tantrum. The lengths he'll go to in order to take Cav down, they're, well, they're a little extreme. But I'm glad I could work with Cav both to get me out of that situation and put a stop to Thomas's vendetta."

"It's totally like some high society elite private school Marvel movie," Dan says, and I swear there are stars in his eyes.

"But seriously," I say. "Connor and I are cool now. I guess it is true what they say about shared experiences bringing people together."

Dan chokes on a fry. "T-Together?" he asks. "Like, *together* together?"

"No, you idiot. I mean like, together as friends."

"Ooooooooooh," he says, as Connor and I look at each other.

We're lost in each other's eyes as the cafeteria door slams open, Thomas standing in the doorway.

"I thought he was out?" Connor asks.

I shrug. "Who knows?"

He comes over to our table.

"Well, well, well, isn't this cozy?" he asks.

I stand up. "What are you doing here?"

"What? You didn't actually think I'd just disappear, did you?"

I shake my head. I didn't think that would be the last time we heard from him, but I kind of hoped it would. "Where have you been?"

He waves a hand. "Oh, you know, here and there."

"That's um, nice."

He nods. "It *is* nice," he says. "I went to Aruba, drank myself stupid, got my dick sucked whenever I wanted, it was great."

"Yeah, sounds like it," I reply.

"And now I'm back."

He takes a seat. "So, who wants to fill me in on what's been happening?"

Connor and I look at each other. Just what is Thomas playing at?

"Er," Pete says. "Not much, I guess."

Thomas looks around. "I see some things have changed," he says. "You part of the group now?" he asks Connor.

Connor shrugs. "I'm just sitting here, eating lunch."

"Yeah," Dan says. "They're like, friends now."

"Friends," Thomas says. "Well isn't that all cozy and shit. Does this mean you've—"

"What do you want, Thomas?" I ask, cutting him off.

"What do I want?" he asks. "What do I *want*? I want a lot of things."

I give him a look.

He laughs and shakes his head. "Cav, Cav, Cav. You need to lighten up, man."

I arch an eyebrow. "Do I?"

"Of course you do."

"Right, because my former best friend showing up out of the blue and acting like nothing has gone on, is totally fine."

Thomas shrugs. "Why not?" He slings an arm around Connor. "If Connor and I are good, then why not everyone else?"

"*Are* you and Connor good?" Pete asks.

Thomas swings his gaze around to him. Pete subsequently ducks his head. "Why wouldn't we be okay?"

"Er, because he dumped you and you didn't take it at all well," Chloe supplies.

"Ah, Fontana," Thomas says. "Tell me, how was your little threesome with our fearless leader here? Earthshattering?"

She puts down her fork. "It was a hell of a lot more satisfying than what I imagine being with you would be like."

There are snickers all around.

Thomas turns back to me. "So you got to her as well."

"Got to her? I haven't gotten to anyone," I tell him.

He sighs. "I was never going to win with you, was I?"

"Win what?" I ask. "We were friends; there was nothing to win."

He shakes his head. "That's what you think." With that, he walks out.

"You're a fucking idiot," I say to Dan as I sit down again.

"What? I was just catching him up."

"By telling him his ex-boyfriend and I are friends? Why would you think that's a good idea with everything that's gone on?"

"Oh, yeah. I didn't think of that. Sorry."

I cuff him over the back of the head.

There's a few minutes silence where I'm sure we're all wondering what the hell that was about and what the fuck Thomas is going to do next.

We don't have to wait long as the teleconferencing system blares to life and Thomas appears on the screen. He looks, well, pissed, like, *super* pissed. I have no doubt that anger is about to be unloaded on me.

"Attention students," he says.

"What is he doing?" Chloe asks.

I shrug and hope like hell I haven't pushed him over the edge.

"It's me, Thomas Rose, recently scorned lover to Connor Siddell and slightly crazy second fiddle to our *esteemed* leader, Cavanaugh McLaughlin. I'm here today to burst that precious bubble our lord and savior has lived in for the entirety of his previous life."

"Holy shit," Chloe whispers as Connor shakes his head. "He's completely lost it, hasn't he?"

Meanwhile, my heart is in my throat. What is Thomas

going to do? Going to say? I don't have anything to hide, well, not after I speak to my parents, but I want to do it on *my* terms.

Under the table, Connor squeezes my thigh.

"A quick show of hands, who here remembers my dear friend Max Emory?" Thomas asks.

Whispers rise around the cafeteria, and people start to look around.

"Don't be scared," Thomas says. "I found a friend, and yes, I do still have one or two of those, who's hacked into the system for me. I can see you, you can see me, but no one, and I mean no one, can stop me. So I'll ask again. Who here remembers my dear friend Max Emory?"

A few hands go up.

"Good, good," Thomas says. "For those of you who don't remember, Max was one of the most promising baseball players Windswept had ever seen. He was incredible. A great talent and an even great friend, isn't that right, Cav?" he asks, looking straight at me.

I don't move.

Thomas continues. "Max was the Curly to Cav's and my Larry and Moe. He was the pepperoni to our pizza, the mustard to our hot dog." He wipes away a nonexistent tear. "And then it all ended over the summer when he killed himself. But do we know *why?*" He scratches at his chin. "You've heard the rumors. We know Cav has taken responsibility for Max's death, but *why?* They were such good friends. What could Cav have done to make Max snap like that? It just doesn't make sense, does it?"

I can feel the weight of a cafeteria's worth of stares.

"Do you want to tell them what happened that night, or should I?" Thomas asks.

I sit there, paralyzed, my breathing shallow and fast, the room spinning around me.

"How about we let me do it, huh?" Thomas says. "Your storytelling lacks a certain… panache."

He kicks back in his seat, putting his feet up on the desk. "Let me set the scene for you, boys and girls. It was the summer before junior year, and yours truly was hosting the party of the season. The drinks were flowing, and good times abounded. But not for you, right, Cav? We all know how Cav likes to stay in control at all times.

"Anyway, the drinks are flowing, and everyone's having a good time. Eventually, as parties do, they wind down, allowing those who want to continue partying the opportunity to… sneak off.

"Our boys Max and Cav were no different, moving to my very comfy pool house."

My blood runs cold. He couldn't know. There's no way he could know. But it explains how he's been able to allude to… things about me.

"Not an original location, but that was exactly what I was hoping when I placed a few cameras in there. You never know what will happen at these types of things, and the internet goes crazy for wasted teenagers making dubious decisions. But this wasn't a dubious decision, was it, Cav?"

The screen flickers, then some seriously good quality footage begins to play. It shows Max kissing me before he backs away, then me grabbing him, palming his dick, and him going to his knees. Some people shake their heads, a few even get up and leave.

"Some interesting viewing, huh?" Thomas asks, switching the visual back to him.

The whispers in the cafeteria get louder. The few teachers who are in here are frantically trying to turn the system off, but to no avail. In the background of the broadcast we can hear and see someone trying to get into the office, but apparently Thomas has locked himself in.

"Cav?" Connor asks, grabbing my arm. "Are you okay?"

But I can't answer. I can't do anything but sit there and watch my world come down around me.

"Don't worry," Thomas says. "It gets better."

He switches back to the footage, showing Max blowing me and my embarrassingly quick climax.

"I have to admit, I did think you'd have a *bit* more stamina," Thomas says, again switching back to himself. "A little excited were we, Cav?"

There are laughs all round. Dan, Pete, the other guys, people I don't know. People I do. The only ones who aren't laughing are me, Connor, Chloe, and Jase.

"I mean, it's not like it was your first time."

My head snaps to the screen.

He laughs and covers his mouth. "Oh, it was? How sweet. Not sure Mommy Dearest would approve of you not saving yourself for marriage, but this isn't the 1950s. Anyway," he continues, "there's some back and forth after that, a few more sweet moments that no one really cares about before we get to the *really* good stuff."

The screen switches again to show me standing

behind Max, plowing into him, jacking him with a vengeance.

I get up, tripping over the bench I'm sitting on in my haste.

"Oh, what's that, Cav?" Thomas asks, freezing the screen on my face right as I come. "Leaving? But we haven't even gotten to the best part."

Connor turns and helps me up, holding my weight, my knees unable to hold it.

"Unfortunately, things didn't end well for my buddies, and our fearless leader, Cav, goes running home like a little girl."

He shows the footage of me leaving, the look of devastation on Max's face clear for all to see.

"But then things take a turn, don't they Cav?"

I'm shaking, Connor holding basically all my weight.

"Just an hour or two after this happens," he switches back to the still of me balls deep in Max, a look of pure bliss on my face, "my dear, dear friend Max is dead, Cav the only 'witness.'"

"I didn't know there were cameras," I murmur.

"What was that?" Connor asks, leaning closer to me.

"I didn't realize there were cameras," I repeat. "He had a gun. I went to talk to him and he...."

"So let's examine that in more detail, shall we?" Thomas says.

The footage shows me and Max outside, and Max pointing the gun at me. It's a little bit grainy and shaky, as if recorded on a cell phone.

Chloe gasps.

"Holy fuck," Connor whispers.

"I didn't… I didn't…."

Eventually we go into the pool house, where the original camera picks up. It shows us sitting on the couch, talking, the gun still in Max's hand.

"I got angry at him," I say. "I said horrible things and hurt him."

"I'm sure you didn't mean it," Connor replies.

I look at him. "But I did."

"Just what did you say to our friend, Cav? What were the last words you said to him? What were the last words Max said? Did he die thinking you were a good guy? Or did he die finally knowing the truth about you, that you're a fake and a phony and, in the end, a murderer."

The footage shows him getting more and more worked up before I hold my hand out for the gun. He cradles it to his chest, and I reach for it.

It's then, finally, blissfully, the broadcast shuts off.

I look around at hundreds of questioning, doubting, accusing glares pointed at me.

CHAPTER 27

Connor and Chloe usher me out of the cafeteria.

"Holy shit," Chloe says. "That was fucked-up."

"He's insane," Connor adds. "Thomas has completely lost it."

"Max's death was ruled a suicide. I don't know why he's bringing that up. Let the guy rest in peace, for fuck's sake," Chloe spits. "And those cameras.... What kind of creep has fucking cameras installed in his pool house so he can spy on people?"

"Thomas," I answer.

She shakes her head. "That is so far beyond fucked up. I don't even know what to say to that."

I shrug. "He wants to feel powerful, like he has something over someone. I'm sure there have been more than a few people who have fallen foul of Thomas and those cameras. How many parties has he had?"

She curses under her breath.

"But I never thought he'd do that to Max, that he'd use Max like this."

"Is that, what um, happened? The reason why you took responsibility for his death?" she asks.

I nod. "He killed himself because of me," I tell him. "He held the gun to his head and fired," I say. I hold my hand to my head, finger pointed at my temple. "Bang."

"I'm sure there was nothing you could've done," Connor consoles. "And if you knew what would happen, you'd take it all back."

I nod. "He was my friend. My… first."

"Ah, shit," Chloe curses again.

"You didn't ask," I point out.

"Ask what?" Connor says.

"If I did it."

"I know you didn't."

"How?"

"Because it's not your style."

"How do you know it's not?" I press.

"I just do."

I stop. "But how?"

He faces me, looking me in the eye. "Because I know you, Cavanaugh McLaughlin. You're the boy who pulled me out of the wreck of my car and sat outside my hospital room even though you knew people would recognize you. You paid my hospital bills and took the blame even though it wasn't yours. You let your parents divorce you, and you're willing to endure more for me. That guy doesn't kill his best friend."

"I'd like to kill Thomas right now."

He laughs. "Get in line, babe."

"What is everyone going to think?" I ask. "I've been so

horrible to everyone, said some really, *really* despicable things. How do I fix that?"

"You fix it one day at a time. You fix it by being honest with yourself, with me, with your parents. Don't worry about anyone else, they don't matter."

"Maybe" I say. I hate how small my voice sounds, but fuck, my world has just come crashing down around me. Surely I'm allowed a little pity. I never thought Thomas would do this. Sure, I pushed him, but he pushed me as well. He knows who I am, knew what I'd do if threatened.

"Did I push Thomas too hard?" I ask as we resume walking to the parking lot.

He sighs. "Maybe?"

My heart sinks.

"I don't know," he continues. "I think you came at him the way you do anyone and how I assume you've come after everyone else. It was certainly how you came after me. I think it would be easy to say, in light of everything that's happened that yeah, you did, but…."

"But what?" I ask.

He runs a hand through his hair. "But I think you had to come at him this hard. The stakes here are high, so fucking high. I mean, he just outed you and indirectly attacked your mom. Even if she is the spawn of Satan, that's heavy."

"Yeah, okay."

"I do think there's no one on this Earth who would've predicted *this* would happen, though."

We finally get to the car, and I lean against it.

"What the fuck am I going to do?" I ask again.

Connor takes my hand and laces his fingers through

mine. "First off, it's *we*, what are *we* going to do, and second, I don't know."

I choke out a laugh and rest my head on his shoulder. "Thanks, babe."

He kisses my ear. "You're welcome."

"Ahem." Chloe clears her throat. "I believe that I am involved in this little threesome as well."

"Haven't you and Cav already had one of those?" Connor asks, arching an eyebrow.

She winks at me. "Don't worry, sugar. Next time, we'll be sure to invite you too."

He laughs and hugs me tighter to him. "No one gets in his pants except me, got it?"

She laughs. "But seriously, what do we do now?" she asks.

I look at Connor, and he raises an eyebrow. "Are you sure you want to get involved in all this?" I question.

"Murder, intrigue, and betrayal? Who *wouldn't* want to be involved?" she replies.

Connor takes her in his arms. "You're the best, Chlo."
She beams.

"This is by no means how I saw my senior year playing out, but it's been interesting."

I shake my head. These two.

"So what's next?"

CHAPTER 28

Next turned out to be eating the delicious meals Manuel had made for me on the weekend and binge watching *Avatar: The Last Airbender* on Netflix.

"I want to do that," Chloe says. "Hop on a flying bison, say 'yip yip,' and get the fuck out of here."

"*You* want to get out of here," I say.

She looks at me. "Yeah, right. Sorry."

She comes over to me and smooshes my face between her palms. "You know everything's going to be okay, right? We *will* get through this, and you two will ride off into the sunset and live happily ever after."

I chuckle as Connor tucks her under his arm and kisses the top of her head.

My phone rings, and I fish it out of my pocket, my father's name flashing on the screen.

"Father," I answer.

"What the hell have you done now?" he asks, not bothering with pleasantries.

"Nothing. Why?"

"I'm getting calls from the school and concerned parents. Something about a relationship?"

"It's um, yeah…." I trail off.

"Is this something the senator and Aiden need to be concerned about? Some kind of liberal conspiracy to disrupt this bill she's working on?"

I blow out a breath, more than a little ashamed that I'm *relieved* he's not listening to what I'm sure many people are telling him. Then again, they've never listened to the rumors about me; convinced they're just that.

"Er…."

"Because I have to tell you, we thought these problems were done with. This is *exactly* why we wanted to distance ourselves from you, so that you would stop causing problems."

I know I should tell him the truth, that this is my perfect opportunity to tell him the truth about me, but not like this. Call me petty, but I really don't want to do this as a direct result of something Thomas did.

"I know, and I'm sorry. Thomas reacted poorly to something at school and lashed out. I'll handle it, it won't be a problem again."

"Our agreement remains intact then?" he asks.

"Yes, it remains intact," I grit out.

"Good."

"Is that all?" I just want this conversation, this day, to be over. I want to curl up with Connor and forget about everything that's happened, and not think about all that's still to come.

"The senator wants me to remind you about the obligations you still have as a McLaughlin."

I pinch the bridge of my nose. "I am well aware of my *obligations*."

"Yes, well, be sure to keep those in mind the next time you decide to play around."

I huff out a breath. "Look, Dad, I've got stuff to do, so unless you have something else to say, I'll see you when the senator's back in town."

With that, I end the call.

"Problem?" Connor asks.

I shake my head. "Not really. That was just a call to remind me of my obligations to the McLaughlin name, and to cover the senator's ass from attacks from 'the liberals who want to take down the senator's latest bill.'"

"Seriously?" Chloe asks.

"God bless them, they've never believed any rumors about me, always attributing them to some kind of conspiracy designed to take her down."

"That is some...." Chloe trails off.

I shrug. "It's the life I lead. The one I've always led. The one I would've had to lead forever if not for...." It's my turn to trail off as I look to Connor.

He swipes his thumb over my cheek and blows me a kiss. "What about Max?" Connor asks.

"They were never bothered by that. The police, DA, and ME all filed their reports, there's nothing to worry about there."

"Do you, um, want to talk about him?" Connor asks. "You've never mentioned him before."

I sigh and run my hand through my hair. "Growing up, it was always Thomas, Max, and me. Max was an incredible ball player, so a lot of his time went to that. He was actually signed to the Iowa Cubs, the Chicago Cubs farm team. He was going to win them another World Series…." I shake my head. "We kind of lost touch a little bit, just because he was so focused. Then Thomas had that party….

"I didn't have any idea Max was gay. Maybe I'd missed the signs or not cared or whatever, but I was surprised when he told me he was interested in me. I was also kind of in awe. It took a hell of a lot of balls to admit that, especially to me, of all people.

"We hooked up, and it was… it was like I'd been living my whole life in the dark and someone turned the lights on. I knew I was gay from an early age, like I'm sure you both did."

They nod.

"But growing up…. Homosexuals are abominations, I was told. They're unnatural, unclean, pedophiles. They corrupt all that is good in the world and will bring us all to the gates of hell. I tried to fight it; I did. But it never worked. I'd watch gay porn, get myself off, and hate myself immediately after. I'd step into scalding-hot showers and watch my skin turn bright red and almost blister. I'd starve myself or break my laptop. Once I even tried to get those chemical castration drugs, but the card was declined because the bank thought it was a fraudulent purchase.

"I tried; I really did. By the time Max came along, I'd given up fighting and was resigned to hating myself for the rest of my life.

"But then Max happened. I told him the same thing I told you," I say to Connor, ignoring the look of devastation on his face. "I told him we couldn't be a thing. I mean, he'd grown up around my parents, he knew what they'd say, what they'd do." Tears roll down my cheeks. Connor scoots next to me, slinging an arm around me, bringing me to his side while Chloe grabs one of my hands.

"We couldn't be together," I say.

"No, you couldn't," Connor confirms.

"But he wouldn't listen. He threatened to out me, and I… I said some horrible things to him. He accused me of being a coward. He was right. I am."

"You were scared, confused," Connor says, cupping my cheek.

"It doesn't excuse what I said, how I acted. He said he hoped what we did haunted me. I guess he'd be happy to know it does."

"I don't think he would," Chloe says. "I don't think he'd be happy he was causing his friend this much pain."

"Do you know the last thing I said before he died?" I ask.

They shake their heads.

"That he was nothing but a fuckup." I chuckle. "The only thing he ever fucked up, the *only* thing, was choosing to love me. Maybe if he hadn't, he'd still be alive."

"It wasn't your fault," Connor says.

I shake my head, and he grips my chin. Hard. "Listen to me, Cav. I'm telling you, it's not your fault. There was nothing you could've done. His mind was made up long before you two hooked up."

"He was my best friend," I say, more tears rolling down my cheeks.

"Oh, babe." He gathers me in his arms. "He always will be. But he was obviously very troubled. I mean, yeah, you're great in bed—"

Chloe makes gagging noises.

"—but not *that* fantastic that I'd kill myself over not having you. That's way past extreme."

"He's right," Chloe says. "I could've done without the bedroom details, but as much as I loved Max, as much as we all did, what he did.... You said he called you a coward?"

I nod.

"I don't want to speak ill of the dead, but I think he was wrong. You're not the coward. You're in the process of coming out, that's not being a coward. That's brave as fuck."

I sigh, and Connor holds me tighter.

"I think," he says, his chest rumbling underneath my ear, "it's unlikely we'll ever come to a consensus about this, so why don't we shelve this talk and try to relax, huh?"

Chloe nods while I snuggle closer, always closer, to Connor.

That night, I fall asleep with my head on his chest, his hands running through my hair.

I couldn't give Max a future, but I'm determined to have one with this boy I've given every reason to hate me.

CHAPTER 29

"Are you okay?" Connor asks as we sit in the Windswept parking lot.

"I don't know," I reply. And I don't. I know it's going to be bad in there, but also, I don't really care. I don't know how I am at all at the moment. I think I'm always going to feel an immense amount of guilt over my involvement with Max and his death. Max was my friend. My lover, even if it was only for a short time. My first. I'll never know if maybe we could've been more or if he'd have moved on and found someone else. And I'm sorry for that. More than he'll ever know. But I've found my way now, I've found it with Connor. And the one thing I do know? Is that I'll never make the same mistake again. I turn to face him. "I wish we could go back to the penthouse, order in, and never leave."

He chuckles, picks up my hand, and gives it a squeeze. "So do I, babe."

I blow out a breath. "We have to go in, don't we?"

"Yeah, we do. But no matter what happens, I'm with you every step of the way, okay?"

I nod. "Thank you. I don't know if I've said it enough, or at all, but thank you for sticking with me. I know I've been… well, an ass but I'm so fucking grateful you're here."

He gives my hand another squeeze. "Me too."

I take a deep breath. "Okay, let's do this."

It kills me not to be able to walk down the hall holding Connor's hand, but he's close enough to brush against me a couple of times, just to let me know he's there. I suppose now that everything I did with Max has been exposed, that's not really necessary, but—

"You know what?" I say, stopping suddenly. "Fuck this."

Connor stops and looks at me, brows furrowed.

"Excuse me, everyone," I call, as if their attention wasn't already on me. "Hi, it's me, Cavanaugh McLaughlin, your resident *not* homophobe. While that tape was a gross invasion of my and Max's privacy, and everyone else that hooked up in that pool house, what you saw was indeed true. Max and I did engage in a casual sexual relationship. That wasn't fake or staged or anything. I am indeed gay and in a very not-casual relationship with Connor Siddell." I grab his hand. "If anyone would like to complain or make comments, I really don't care." Pulling Connor to me, I kiss him. Hard. And as if I needed a sign we're meant to be, he kisses me back just as hard, meeting me stroke for stroke.

When we finally break apart, I'm sure the goofy grin he wears is mirrored on my face. He presses one more kiss to my lips, which I take further, then moves to walk beside me, my arm slung over his shoulders, his around my waist. We pass a multitude of faces, some shocked, some taken aback, some disgusted, some happy, and some... jealous? But I couldn't give a fuck. I have the guy of my dreams in my arms and I couldn't be happier. Nothing can take this feeling away from me.

CHAPTER 30

L ater that day, Connor and I are summoned to the Principal's office.

"Any idea what this is about?" he asks, taking my hand and pulling me to him.

"I can guess," I say before kissing him. Fuck, it feels amazing to do this, to be with him. We may not be able to walk around Millennium Park like this *just* yet, but this, being here, it's like a trial run and I'm loving it.

"Want to share with the class?" he asks before taking my lips again.

"Not really. I'd much rather get the fuck out of here and not worry about any of this."

He chuckles as someone clears their throat.

"Gentlemen," Principal Harrison says. "If you'll follow me?"

I sigh and drop my arms from around Connor. "Come on, let's get this over with."

"Take a seat," the principal says.

We duly sit.

"I wanted to bring you both in as some, ah, *news* has reached me of your... relationship. From what I saw just now, I see those reports are correct."

I hide my smile as Connor sits forward in his seat. Windswept is officially a nondenominational academy, but it doesn't mean they're liberal. Or tolerant, apparently.

"Do you mean to tell me," Connor says, "that you've called us in because we're in a relationship?"

"Now, we're very clear on the displaying of relationships—"

"So is the Supreme Court," Connor hits back. "Tell me, is it *all* relationships that bother you, or just the homosexual ones? 'Cause I have to say, I've seen more than my fair share of PDA from heterosexual couples, and no one's ever had a problem with them. You also didn't have a problem with me when I was with Thomas Rose. So I have to ask, is it a problem with the relationship or the people in said relationship?"

The principal looks to me. "We are simply trying to protect your... modesty," he says.

I chuckle. "I think I lost my modesty a long time ago, but if you're calling me in here as a favor to my parents, you can save it."

"Cavanaugh, you *must* be aware that something like... *this* won't stay quiet."

"And you have to know that I'm well aware of that."

"If this is a phase—"

I scoff.

"—or some sort of attempt at attention seeking—"

"I just had a *rather* intimate moment broadcast to the

entire school. I think I'm good with the attention seeking," I say. "But since you mention attention seeking, what are you going to do about Thomas Rose?"

The principal shifts in his seat. "Well, as you'd expect, Thomas will ah, of course, be ah, facing some kind of sanction."

"Some kind of sanction," I repeat. "Well, that screams of a swift, authoritative response."

"Cavanaugh—"

"Principal Harrison," I say, cutting him off. "Thomas broadcast what amounts to child porn in your very school. I can't imagine that would be great for your reputation if that were to get out."

"Yes, well…."

"Why hasn't anyone done anything about Thomas?" Connor asks.

The principal shifts in his seat.

"I mean," Connor continues. "What he did was *so* much more outrageous than Cav and I being in a relationship, so that would obviously be your primary concern, right?"

I have to hide my laugh. Watching Connor take it to Principal Harrison is hot as fuck and turning me on something fierce.

"Yes, of course. And as soon as we are able to locate Mr. Rose, he will face the full force of the Windswept honor code."

I nod, trying to keep a straight face. It doesn't surprise me that Thomas has gone MIA again. It's exactly the kind of wimpy behavior that I expect from him.

"But in the meantime," Principal Harrison goes on.

"We need to address the two of you and your... state of mind."

I outright laugh at this. "We're gay, Principal Harrison, that's all. We're good," I tell him.

"But since you seem to be on a mental health kick, it is worth noting LGBTQ kids *do* have a higher instance of suicide," Connor adds. "Perhaps you could think about instituting a program for actual at-risk kids."

Principal Harrison's face gets red. "Yes, well, I think that might be something we could look into. In the, ah, future."

I shake my head. Typical. I don't know what's worse, the senator who's an out-and-out bigot, or the ones here who pretend they're not, but underneath it all, are right there with her.

"Is there anything else?" I ask.

"We would like to... ask you to be... discreet. We wouldn't want the other students getting... ideas."

"Like they're free to be who they want to be and free to love whomever they choose?" Connor asks.

"Can we depend on *your* discretion?" I ask. While I don't fear my parents finding out about me, I do think the decent thing to do would be to tell them myself.

The principal nods. "But, ah, will you...?" He trails off.

"I'll be speaking to my parents as soon as the senator is back from Washington," I tell him.

He nods.

"If this is a phase—"

"It's not," I say, my face hard.

"Even so, I would urge you to carefully consider how it is you will proceed. Your mother is a wonderful woman and has done a lot for the state and indeed the country. I would hate for her reputation and standing to be affected by nothing more than a fling."

I grab Connor's hand, lacing his fingers with mine. "With all due respect, Principal Harrison, you don't know shit. Connor and I are in love, have been for a while now. I love him, he loves me, we're going to ride off into the sunset together and all that bullshit. The senator is not a great woman. She's a bigot and is only out for herself. But I'm sure she'll love to hear that you admire her so. I would caution *you* though to keep that under wraps. You wouldn't want your redneck to show now, would you?"

With that, Connor and I get up and walk out. We keep walking all the way to the parking lot.

"Unlock the door," Connor orders when we get to my car.

I do so, and he opens the back door, shoving me in.

"Ow! What the fuck, Connor!" I ask as I scramble to right myself.

He dives in after me, going straight for my fly. "That was so fucking hot," he says, his hand slipping under the band of my boxer briefs and taking hold of my now rapidly hardening dick.

"Seriously?" I ask as he pumps me.

He grabs my hand and puts it on his boner trying to push through his slacks. "Fuck yes."

"Well, all right then." I chuckle.

"Seriously, babe, you fucking nailed him! And that bit about not showing his redneck? Classic."

"Fucking bastard," I mutter. "You know why he called us in there? 'Cause he's a homophobic bastard. He knows exactly the kind of power I have here and doesn't want Windswept to be known as a school for gays."

"Whatever. Can we not talk about him right now?"

I quirk an eyebrow at him. "You know there is one surefire way to get me to shut up, don't you?" I look at my dick in his hand.

He gives me a lopsided grin before lowering his head and taking me to the back of his throat.

"Holy fuck!" I yell, my hand hitting the roof of my car, the other going to his head and his thick, luscious hair. "Oh God, baby."

"Mmm," he moans around me, sucking me in just the right way.

"Fuck, I love your mouth."

He lets me go with a *pop*. "That's the second time you've said that word."

"Huh?" I ask.

"That's the second, or I guess the third time you've said the L-word. It turns me on."

"The.... Oh!" My cheeks heat. "Well, you did say you wouldn't be the first one to say it."

"And technically you haven't. Not directly *to* me, anyway."

I grab his face and drag him up my body. "Connor Nathan Siddell, I'm in love with you. I love you heart, body, and soul, and if you don't go back to sucking my dick in three seconds, I'm going to lose my shit."

He chuckles and kisses me quickly. "So fucking romantic."

I push his head down.

He laughs some more but doesn't budge. "Hang on. I want to say something."

I roll my eyes but relent. For the time being.

"We didn't have the most straightforward start to our relationship, and it hasn't been smooth sailing, like, at all, but I wouldn't change it for the world."

"Now who's being romantic?" I ask.

He gives my dick a stroke, and I swear my eyes roll to the back of my head. "Be nice."

"You're evil."

"Yeah, but you just told me you love me, so too fucking bad."

"Ugh!" I rub my hands over my face.

He pulls them away. "I love you, Cavanaugh James McLaughlin. And even though you might be mean and evil and all types of a bastard, I don't care, 'cause you're mine."

I grab him and kiss him. Hard. Our teeth clash, tongues duel, and hands go everywhere. It's messy, but it's powerful and it's us. Us.

Eventually we pull apart, and I rest my forehead on his. "You're amazing, you know that?"

He chuckles and gives me a chaste kiss. "Right back atcha."

"You know what would make you even more amazing?" I ask.

"What?"

"If you finally finished sucking my dick."

He outright laughs as he slithers down my body again before sucking my brains, and my heart, out through my dick.

CHAPTER 31

"Are you okay?" I ask as I wipe my mouth as Connor lies panting at the other end of my back seat.

"I can't feel my toes," he says.

"What?" I jump up, well, as much as I can. "Are you okay? Do I need to get you to the hospital? Are you hurt anywhere else?" I start grabbing his arms, shoulders, chest, head, trying to make sure I haven't fucked him up more than I already have.

He grabs my hand. "Hey. Relax. I'm fine; that was just a *really* good blowjob."

I collapse back into my corner. "Don't scare me like that."

He chuckles as he tucks himself away before sliding next to me. "I'm sorry, babe. I didn't think you'd take it that way." He picks up my hand and kisses it.

"In case you haven't noticed, I'm a little sensitive when it comes to you."

He tries to hide his smile but can't. It takes over his whole face and is nothing short of… breathtaking.

I cup his cheek. "We're almost there, aren't we?"

He turns his head to kiss my palm. "Yeah, we are."

"Did you ever think we'd end up here?"

He considers for a second. "Truthfully? No. I hoped we would, but…."

"But what?" I ask.

"Can I be honest?"

"Always."

"Like, *brutally* honest?"

I lean forward and kiss him once. Twice. Three times. "Always," I repeat.

He blows out a breath. "Okay then. Yes, I wanted us to be together, but I honestly didn't know if you would ever let us."

I nod. "That's fair."

"I don't know if you realize what a massive thing you're doing. It was okay for me, 'cause my parents already knew, but yours? Fuck, baby, I am so in awe of you."

I look down at my hand, now holding his in our laps.

He rubs his thumb across my knuckles. "I know you think you're doing this for us, for me, but this is all for you. I'm just the reward."

I look up, and he wiggles his eyebrows.

"You're really okay?" I ask.

"I'm really okay," he confirms. "And once I get the okay from my doctors, you better clear your schedule, 'cause we're spending all day in bed."

My dick jerks as I groan and lean my forehead on his shoulder. "You can't say stuff like that to me when we can't follow through."

"Delayed gratification," he whispers in my ear. "It'll make everything worthwhile, I promise."

The bell rings, breaking our reverie.

"I suppose we should get back in there," I say.

"I suppose we should," he agrees. "But are you okay with everything that's gone down today? You know, in the hall, just now in Principal Harrison's office?"

I blow out a breath. "Principal Harrison can eat a bag of dicks as far as I'm concerned."

At this, he snorts.

"As for everyone else? I knew it would be... an adjustment. But as long as I have you, I can get through it."

He kisses the back of my hand. "You told me you love me, then blew my mind. I think it's safe to say you've got me."

The cafeteria is packed when we get there, conversations slowly stopping as we walk the lunch line, laughing and joking as if I haven't just turned everything on its head.

"Where have you guys been?" Chloe demands, stomping up to us.

"We had a meeting with Principal Harrison," I say. "And then...."

"And then we had a... private meeting," Connor finishes for me.

"You totally fucked in the janitor's closet, didn't you?" she asks, hands on hips.

"Blowjobs in the parking lot," Connor corrects. "He," he nods to me, "won't let me fuck him—"

"Or me fuck him," I interject.

"—until I get the all clear from my docs." He pouts.

I put an arm around him and pull him to me, his back to my front. I kiss his neck. "He's precious cargo."

"Barf," Chloe says and pretends to vomit.

We both laugh, and I let him go, no matter how much I don't want to.

"What's the reaction been like?" I ask her, nodding to the seating area, where all eyes are on us.

She shrugs. "Some are okay, some are acting like it's the most revolutionary thing ever, going on and on about how *brave* you are," she rolls her eyes, "but most don't care."

"And the ones who *do* have a problem?" I ask.

"Fuck 'em," she says, shrugging.

"That easy, huh?"

"Who you are hasn't changed. You're still Cavanaugh McLaughlin, so show them that. And know that Connor and I will be there to back you up. Besides, we all know how scrappy I can get."

We all laugh and head over to my usual table.

There are plenty of looks and whispers, but I keep my head high. I'm Cavanaugh McLaughlin, bad boy of Windswept Academy. I don't take shit from *anybody*.

"You can't be serious," Dan says as we sit down.

"Why can't I?" I ask, folding my hands in front of me.

"Because he's…. You're…. It's just not right."

"Says you."

"So did you," Pete says. "On numerous occasions we had to listen to you spew hate about gays and how it's not natural, how they're not natural, how they should be shot and so on and so forth."

I nod. "I did say that. I didn't mean it, but it doesn't take away from the fact those words did come out of my mouth."

"And?" he asks.

"And I'm sorry. I was going through some shit. Clearly."

"So what? We're supposed to just accept you and all your... new discoveries?" Dan asks.

"You don't have to do shit," I tell him. "But because you're a little bitch without an original thought in your head, you will."

There's a chorus of "ooooooohs."

"I'm gay," I say. "Like it, don't like it, I don't give a fuck. But nothing has changed. *I* haven't changed. Question me again and see how far it gets you."

Dan sits back and scoffs. "Yeah, what are you going to do?"

"You testing me?" I ask.

He shrugs. "What if I am?"

I get up and walk around the table. I come up beside him, bending over so I can speak in his ear, hand on the back of his neck.

"You think you can challenge me?" I ask. "You think you're a big enough man to take *me* on?"

"Yeah, I do."

"You think because I like dick that that makes me soft? Less of a man, right? I mean, I've said as much before, haven't I?"

He nods. "I learned from the best."

"You did, but obviously not enough." I grab the back of his head and slam it into the table.

"Whoa!" everyone calls, most getting up from the table… except Connor and Chloe, who continue to eat their lunch.

"I may have had his dick in my mouth ten minutes ago," I say, loud enough for the whole room to hear me, "but that doesn't mean I'm less of a man."

"If anything," Chloe says through a mouthful of sushi, "it should make you *more* of one, 'cause you know, there's two dicks involved…. Yeah, I'll shut up now."

Connor and I both look at her.

She shrugs. "What? It's true."

"I mean, technically," Connor agrees.

I roll my eyes. "If you two are done?" I ask.

"Oh yeah, sorry," Chloe says. "Continue being all mean and bad and menacing."

Connor nods. "You're doing great, baby. Very scary. Ten out of ten would avoid, you know, that is, if I didn't want to jump your bones right now."

"You three are fucking inthane," Dan says, trying and failing to staunch the flood of blood coming from his nose.

"All the more reason not to fuck with us, huh?" Connor asks.

"Or what?" Dan says. "What are you going to do to me? Kill me, juth like he did Maxth?"

"Max's death was a tragedy," I tell him. "Plain and simple. Was I wrong to take responsibility for it? Maybe. I *did* feel responsible for it. I think I always will. But I didn't pull the trigger."

"And you exthpect uth to beweive that?" Dan asks.

"I don't care what you believe."

He laughs. "You're Cavanaugh McLaughlin, how hard would it be to pay the polithe, the DA, the ME, all of them off? I'm thure there'th more than a few people around town more than happy to have the honorable Thenator McLaughlin owe them a favor."

I sigh. "Yeah, okay, you got me. I *did* kill Max, *and* I paid off them all off. I've got deep pockets and even deeper connections, don't forget that." I was obviously *too* convincing when I was telling people about Max, but honestly, how stupid do you have to be to think a high school kid had enough power to keep himself out of jail for murder? And if they still want to believe that when they all but saw the moment of truth? All power to them. I know what happened. The authorities know. And most importantly, Connor knows.

"You think you're tho powerful—"

"Didn't we just establish I am?" I ask. I sigh. "Get the fuck out of here and don't go saying shit. I hear it all, and I can guarantee it won't end up as... pleasant as this, next time."

Dan shoves back from the table, grabbing his book bag and stalking from the room.

"Anyone else want to try me?" I ask.

The room stays silent.

"I thought not."

"*That* was pleasant?" Connor asks, as I take my seat.

I shrug. "I could've cut his nuts off; can't imagine that would be pleasant."

"No, definitely *not* pleasant," he agrees.

"You think that'll work?" Chloe asks.

"I guess we'll just have to wait and see."

CHAPTER 32

"So this is my room, which, of course, you've already seen," Connor says, leading me in.

"I didn't say so before, but I will now. *That* is going to be a problem." I point to the Lions poster on the far wall.

"I told you, I will support the Cubs or whoever, but NFL is nonnegotiable."

I chuckle, stepping closer to him, drawing him into my arms. "Guess it's a good thing I love you then, huh?" I know it's only been a few hours, but it still gives me a thrill to say those words, something I never thought I would. I never thought I would ever be... free to live my life, love who I wanted. But now that I am.... It feels incredible. It feels like anything is possible, that I can do anything I want.

I know I still have to talk to my parents, but what more can they do? They've already cut me off and probably marked me out of the family Bible, so what do I have to lose? Nothing. I've only got things I can gain, and I gained big with Connor.

And judging by the smile on his face, I hope he feels the same.

"Is it stupid how much I love hearing that?" he asks.

I shake my head. "Only if it's stupid how much I love saying it."

"I love you," he whispers before he leans up and kisses me.

We've just gotten to the good part, our tongues dancing, hands undoing each other's shirts, when there's a knock on the door.

Connor rests his head on my chest. "I'm beginning to think the universe is against us having some quality time," he says.

I push back his hair. "We had quality time today, you know, in the back of my car."

He groans as whoever it is knocks again. "But I need more."

I kiss his forehead. "Soon, baby, I promise."

He sighs, but calls "come in."

Jase peers around the door. "Is this, um, a bad time?"

I scoot back on the bed. "Nah, man, come on in."

He comes and sits on the end of the bed.

"What's up?" Connor asks.

"So are you two like, totally together and everything now?"

Connor nods. "Yeah, we are. Are you... okay with that?"

I'm not going to lie, I'm a little bit pissed Connor is asking Jase that, but I know Connor values Jase's opinion. I also know that Jase is uber protective of his older brother and has been iffy on our relationship from the start.

Jase looks to me. "You love my brother?"

I nod. "With all my heart."

"And you won't hurt him?"

"Hurting him is the very last thing I ever want to do." I take a breath. "I know our relationship didn't start out in the best of ways. I was afraid, of a lot of things. But your brother has shown to me just how far I will go for someone I love." I grab Connor's hand. "He's also shown me what it feels like to love someone, and have someone love me. I promise you, and him, that I will look after him, that I will love him for the rest of my life."

Jase nods. "What are you guys going to do about Thomas?"

I blow out a breath and run a hand over my head. "We'd have to find him first. According to Principal Harrison he's gone MIA again."

"He's not a good guy," Jase says.

"No, he's not. And I'm sorry he was ever a part of your lives."

"I want him to go away and never come back," he says.

Connor grabs his hand and squeezes. "I'm pretty sure we all do."

"I mean, personally I'd like to see him suffer, maybe spend some time in prison, or you know, meet the business end of a two by four, but…. What?" I ask when I see Connor's face.

He shakes his head, a smile on his face though. "Still the bad boy, huh?"

I cup his cheek. "I'm sorry to tell you, babe, but I think

the bad boy is always going to be a part of me. You definitely tamed him, but he'll never be completely gone."

"Annnnnnnd that's my queue to leave," Jase says, getting up.

"But we're okay, aren't we?" I ask before he leaves.

He looks at me, then to his brother. "I can see you love my brother. I saw it before you guys were even together. That's all I want, is for him to be happy. You make him happy."

I nod. "Thanks, man."

"You two deserve to be happy, so be happy."

Connor lets go of my hand and wraps his arm around me. "We will."

That was the plan, anyway.

CHAPTER 33

"**D**o you think we're finally rid of Thomas?" Connor asks as we lie in my bed later that night.

After Jase's interruption, as lovely and cathartic as it was, we wanted privacy so Connor packed a bag, and we came to the penthouse.

I sigh running my hand up and down his side. "I hope so, but knowing Thomas as I do, I doubt he'd be satisfied with all the damage he's done. He'd want to annihilate me completely."

Connor blows out a breath. "How is it possible for one person to be so set on destruction?"

I run a hand over my head. "A lot of it is probably my fault," I say. "Growing up, because of who the senator is, I got a lot of attention, a lot of people sucked up to me." I chuckle. "I got away with a lot of shit. I can see how that would breed animosity."

"Animosity, yes, but the desire to bring you down completely?"

I shrug. "I'm a bastard. A lot of people probably think I deserve it. And maybe I do."

He hugs me tighter. "I don't think you're a bastard."

"But you did once, didn't you? When I was horrible to you when you first came to Windswept?"

"I don't know if I ever thought you were a bastard," he says. "I think I thought you were lost and I definitely wanted to help you find yourself, but a bastard? Not quite."

I chuckle and kiss his chin. "So my reputation doesn't bother you?" I ask. It's something that I have been wondering for a while, and a question I truly want an answer to.

"If that bothered me, I wouldn't be here, in your arms, half naked and trying to think of anything but the time when we can spend all day here, fucking each other's brains out."

"Well, now that's all I can think of. Thanks."

He chuckles and presses a kiss against my pec. "We're in this together, babe. For better or worse."

"For better or worse," I echo.

CHAPTER 34

The following morning we're woken by my phone ringing at the buttcrack of dawn. Connor groans and hides his face in between my neck and shoulder. I kiss the back of his head as I reach for the object of our rude awakening.

"What?" I snap, not even bothering to look at who's calling, but knowing it could only be a few people.

"Is that how you answer the phone to your betters, boy?" my father growls.

I blow out a breath. "It is when they call at whatever ungodly hour this is."

"It's 5:00 A.M. and the early editions of the *Chicago Sun Times* have already been circulating for hours."

"Good for them, but why are you calling *now* to tell me that? Furthermore, why is it even relevant knowledge for me to have?"

"It's relevant," he grits out, "because once again there is a liberal conspiracy against you, taking up space and attention."

I bolt up, Connor groaning again and rolling away from me.

"What?" I ask.

"It appears one of your classmates, or maybe a scorned lover perhaps, I don't know, nor do I really care, has gone to Stuart White of the *Sun Times* and told him *all* about your love life. Your *homosexual* love life."

"Holy fuck," I swear.

"Yes, indeed."

"Does it say who the source is?" I ask, reaching for my iPad.

"Why, yes, Cavanaugh, it does. In block letters of the article it says 'by the way, my source is Joe Schoolboy, aged seventeen. They live at this address.'"

"Holy fuck," I say again. I manage to pull up the article in question and poke Connor, muting my dad's call. "Babe, wake up."

He groans and scrubs a hand over his face. "I don't wanna."

"I, we, I've got a major fucking problem."

"Huh?"

"Cavanaugh? Are you still there?" my dad asks.

"Just a second, I'm reading the article now." I mute him again.

"Article?" Connor asks. "What article?"

"Someone went to the *Sun Times* and outed me," I tell him. Really, outing me is a kind way of putting it, and it's not even the worst part, it's just kind of... a side effect of the article.

It's a gossip piece, because no real journalist would publish these claims with their byline on it. But Stuart

White, who obviously thinks the *Sun Times* doesn't hit hard enough, has no problems doing so, his byline complete with headshot proudly displayed at the top of the gossip page. And underneath… well, it's nothing short of a scandal. The senator is going to be furious. This is going to take all the attention off her and her precious bill and put it squarely onto me.

The column details Max's and my relationship in full. It then adds in Connor's accident and our tumultuous relationship prior to us getting together.

"Holy fuck," I say yet again. I feel it'll be a phrase I utter a lot in the coming hours, maybe even days.

"What?" Connor asks, now sitting up.

I hand him the iPad.

"I thought we had an agreement," my dad says. "The senator cannot afford to be distracted right now. This is a distraction, Cavanaugh."

"I did have an agreement," I reply. "And I was sticking to it."

"Obviously you didn't."

I scrub a hand over my face. "I'll fix it."

"See that you do, please."

"But um, about what the article says…."

"The senator would prefer I wait to discuss it until she's back from DC. She'll be here in a few hours."

"Oh. Is she…. Did she…. Is this going to set her back too much?" As much as the senator's beliefs anger and disgust me, she's still my mom, and she's worked hard to get where she is. Though they say the opposite, Washington is still a boys' club, and she's had to fight for everything she has. While I may not have fond feelings for the senator the last thing I want is for my actions to jeopardize her career. It's one of the reasons I was okay with our "arrangement." The more distance between her and my… relationships, the better. For both of us.

"Aiden is working to limit it. Even if the column is taken down, word will still get around."

"Right."

"It goes without saying that we would like you to stay silent on the matter until we can get some… cooperation from the *Sun Times*."

"Of course."

"And if you're able to compile a list of names you think could be the source, that would also be beneficial."

"Right, I'll get on it."

"And Cavanaugh?"

"Yes?"

"If you do have a… friend there, it would also be beneficial if they don't say anything either. I know the senator would feel better if you had them sign an NDA, but I suppose the damage is done now."

An NDA? Holy fuck. Can I even ask Connor to sign one? *Should* I?

"I'll be in touch once the senator lands. Try not to stuff anything up in the meantime." With that, he ends the call.

"Holy shit," Connor says, looking up from the iPad.

"I know."

"Your dad?" he asks.

I nod.

"He pissed?"

"Umm." I pause. "More like resigned, I think. Like he always thought one day I'd fuck up their lives this bad."

"And your mom?"

"On her way from Washington. I'm not to speak to anyone or do anything except file a lawsuit against the columnist and paper and, um, have you sign an NDA. But I'm not going to do that, so don't even think about it," I say in a rush.

He throws his head back. "An NDA? That is so... Washington."

I shrug. "I'm not going to have one drawn up, so you don't need—"

He holds a hand up. "I'll sign it."

"What?"

It's his turn to shrug. "I'll sign it. If that's what your parents need to convince them I'm not a threat, then I'll do it. It's not a big deal to me."

I tackle him and kiss him deeply. "Thank you," I say, looking into his ice-blue eyes.

He shrugs. "I'm not planning on speaking to the media, would *never* speak to them media, so what does it matter?"

I kiss him again.

"My father wants a list of names," I tell him.

"Names?"

"Yeah, people I think might be the source."

"Well, I think it's safe to say Thomas is at the top of it."

I groan and rest my forehead on his shoulder. "I shouldn't have gone after him like I did."

Connor runs his hands through my hair. "You had to show everyone they couldn't fuck with you. Plus, you said yourself that he was never going to be satisfied until he took you down."

"Still, I didn't *have* to go after him like I did. I didn't have to push him this far."

He lifts my head up. "Yeah, you did. Whether you want to admit it or not, there was a weakness, an opening. You had to shut that shit down. The way the student body functions is because you keep it in line. Is it perfect? No, but what school is? You *had* to do what you did."

I slump down on him, rolling so I'm pressed to his side. "I hate this."

"I know," he says, pressing a kiss to my forehead.

Just then my phone beeps with a message. I grab it, only to see a smiling Thomas on some beach somewhere, the gossip page of the *Sun Times* open on his iPad, a huge smile on his face.

CHAPTER 35

"Holy shit," I say, my phone gripped tight in my hand.

"You've got to be joking," Connor says.

"I don't think he is."

"I can't believe he did this."

"Can't you?" I ask, flopping back on the bed. "Because I can."

"He seriously went to the paper?"

"He seriously went to the paper," I confirm.

"What are you going to do?"

"I don't know what I can do. I mean, I can call and try to get them to take the piece down, but I don't know if they would actually do it."

"It's worth a try, right?"

"I guess." I start googling the editor of the *Sun Times*. I finally manage to find a number and get through to a snooty assistant, who when she realizes who I am, puts me through to his private line.

The editor answers the call much like I answered the one from my father.

"Here's the deal," I tell him once I get the pleasantries out of the way. "You take the column down, issue an apology, and censure your… reporter. In return, I'll give you a very nice donation. How does that sound? I'll also try to keep the senator's wrath off you, although I can't promise that."

"Now just wait a min—"

"There will be no waiting," I tell him. "Your paper published a major intrusion into my privacy and didn't even bother to reach out to me for comment. You know this is fucked-up but don't want to look like you're being pushed around by an eighteen-year-old. I get it. You have a reputation to uphold, but keep that in mind. By now I'm sure you're being inundated by calls from the senator's chief-of-staff. If it makes you feel better to make it look like you're agreeing to his demands when you've already decided to do with mine, then that's fine. Just get it done."

"How much of a nice donation?" he asks.

I chuckle. "A *very* nice one. You want to send your kid to college? Consider it done."

There's silence for a while before he says "done."

"Good," I say. "But don't feel bad if you make Aiden work for a little bit." I end the call.

Connor chuckles. "Just couldn't help yourself, could you?"

I shrug. "You have to look for positives in everything, right?"

He kisses my shoulder. "Are you okay?"

"Well, it's not quite the way I had planned to come out, but there's no denying it's effective."

"What did your dad say?"

"He still thinks it's some kind of liberal conspiracy, but I think he also might think there's some truth to it."

"How do you think the senator will take it?"

"Honestly? I don't know. Badly probably. But also, they don't have much to do with me anymore, so she may not care that much. I'm also legally an adult, so there's not much she *can* do."

"What about what they said about Max?" he asks. We've talked at length about it, but he obviously still worries about me.

"There's always going to be guilt there. I think I'm always going to think I could've done more. I *should've* done more."

"And what is the more you could've done?" he asks.

"I wouldn't have said the stuff I said. I would've made more of an effort to be with him, put more thought into our relationship."

"No, you wouldn't," he says. "Your guilt is saying you would have, but that's not you, Cav. You weren't ready to have a relationship with Max; you were barely ready to have one with me, and we all know I'm irresistible."

I snort but am glad for the slight injection of humor.

"You weren't ready, Cav, and that's nobody's fault."

I sigh and snuggle into his side. "Why is everything so hard?" I ask.

"I'll give you hard," he says, lifting his hips.

I laugh and slap his stomach, taking care to avoid his now healed wound sites.

He chuckles. "But seriously? It's hard because we're different, because we're going against the norm. People don't like that. That's not our fault, it's theirs."

"What do you think will happen now?"

"Well, eventually you're going to have to answer your phone that's going crazy that we've been ignoring."

I chuckle again.

"Then you're going to need to talk to your parents. I can't imagine it's going to be pretty, but then I don't think it ever was going to be. They'll probably rant, they'll rave, they'll try to shame you, and you'll let them. And once they're done, you'll get up and walk out."

"Just like that, huh?"

"It's not like they can do anything to you. You're over eighteen, and they've cut you off in all but name. What's left? Besides, if they try anything, I'll be on their assess."

"You will, huh?"

He presses a kiss to my forehead. "Yeah, I will."

"Will you come with me?" I ask. I hate how small my voice sounds, but I want Connor with me. No, I *need* him with me.

"If you want me to come I will," he says. "But you don't need me there."

I open my mouth to retort, but he continues.

"You *want* me there as support, and that's huge and I love you for it, and if that's what you truly want, of course I'll go, but don't fool yourself into thinking that you can't do this on your own, 'cause you can."

I blow out a breath. "This is going to majorly suck."

He laughs, picks up my hand, and kisses the back of it. "I know it is, but it's the very last thing you need to do, and then you're free. Free, baby. We'll be able to live our lives the way *we* want to, free from worry about what they're going to think, free from hiding. It'll just be us."

"Just us. I like the sound of that."

He kisses me on the mouth this time. "All us, all the time, baby. Count on it."

My phone rings again, and with a sigh, I answer it.

CHAPTER 36

The McLaughlin mansion looks the same as it always has as it looms in front of us. I don't know why I'd think it would be any different. Maybe it's me who's different.

I never thought I'd get out of there. I guess I figured I'd be trapped in its—in their—clutches for the rest of my life.

But I'm free. There's nothing they can say or do to me now that will force me to bend to their will. Not anymore.

Connor squeezes my hand. "I'll be waiting for you right here, okay?" he asks. "Keep your phone in your hand and if you need me, call me and I'll be there straight away."

I lean over, cup his cheek before kissing him. "Thank you."

He squeezes my hand again. "You don't need to thank me," he says. "You're going to be fine. There's going to be a bit of unpleasantness, but once you get that out of the way, we'll be free to live our lives."

I close my eyes, picturing it.

"We're almost there, baby." It's his turn to kiss me, but it's me who deepens it, his tongue matching me stroke for stroke.

He moans and I know I have to stop before we get carried away and instead drive home so I can give Connor the best blowjob of his life.

"I'll be back soon," I say as we break the kiss, but not before I give him another quick peck. I can't help myself, and the best thing is, I don't have to.

I don't bother knocking, instead waltzing in. The senator, my father, and the senator's chief-of-staff are in one of the reception rooms off the main foyer, waiting for me.

"Cavanaugh," the senator says, her arms crossed, mouth tight.

"I'm not talking in front of him," I reply, nodding to Aiden. "This isn't a political matter, so I don't need your handler here to make sure your image is intact."

To be honest, I couldn't care less if Aiden is here or not. I just want to see how easily I can push them.

The senator nods at him, and he gets up with a huff. "You stupid kid," he hisses as he walks past. "Do you have any idea how big you owe me today?"

I chuckle. "I don't owe you shit, but I'm guessing you owe the editor of the *Sun Times* big."

He continues to mutter to himself as he exits the room.

"Need I remind you that Aiden is *my* staff member," the senator says, "and *not* here to clean up your messes?"

"I didn't need him to clean up my mess," I counter. "It's not my fault his homophobic ass probably went in all guns blazing, not bothering to ask if a deal had already been struck to rescind the article."

"Aiden is a good, God-fearing Christian," the senator argues.

"Well, for a good, God-fearing Christian, he's certainly well versed at ass kissing, I'll give him that."

"Aiden has been a loyal aide to the senator for fifteen years," my father reminds me.

"And I'm sure they've probably been fucking for at least fourteen of those."

My father's face goes bright red, while the senator shifts in her seat. Interesting. I'm pretty sure adultery is against the Bible, but that's not my problem.

I sigh. "Why don't we stop pussyfooting around," I say. "Let's get right to it. I have shit to do today."

"Cavanaugh," my father starts, no doubt to admonish me, while the senator says, "Is it true? Are all the rumors true?"

I nod. "They are."

"So you're gay."

"I am."

My father shakes his head.

"And the events that are detailed in the article, they all happened?"

"They did."

"You are aware that the Bible considers your behavior sinful."

"I could give a fuck about that right now," I tell them.

"Cavanaugh…," My father says again.

"Is that all?" I ask

"It's unnatural and against God," the senator continues.

"Anything else?"

"You are an abomination and are going to hell."

I sigh and examine my nails. "And?" I swear I could've written this word for word before I even got here. I want to say what they're saying hurts, but it also kind of doesn't. What they're saying, it doesn't matter to me anymore.

"And?" my father splutters. "Cavanaugh, you are a stain on this family, not to mention the damage you have done to your mother's reputation and campaign."

"The *senator*," I correct, "has never been my mother, much like you've never been my father. Let's not pretend that I'm anything but a prop for your happy family charade."

"It is against God's will—"

"Would you quit with the God's will crap?" I snap at the senator. "It might work for your base, but it has zero play here."

The senator nods. "All right. You are an embarrassment to this family. We have raised you to be elite, to have every door opened for you, for you to want for nothing, and you do *this* to us?"

"First of all, contrary to what you might think, I didn't do *this*, be homosexual, on purpose. Much like you two didn't choose to be heartless bastards, I didn't choose to be gay. I was born this way." I sigh. "I know I've put you through a lot in the past, some of which *was* on purpose, but you have to admit, you did ask for it."

They sit, unmoved.

"But none of this is your concern, is it?" I ask. "You washed your hands of me, and I am no longer your problem."

"It's our problem when it makes the goddamn paper and takes time and attention away from the senator and her work," my father spits. "She does not deserve to be treated this way."

"So tell them the truth," I respond. "Tell them what awesome parents you are and have nothing to do with me. Or tell them that I'm a well-known fuckup and you pray for my salvation. I honestly don't give a fuck what you do, and you don't have to give a fuck what I do. We were nothing more than a convenience for each other," I tell them. "And now our usefulness has been used up." I run a hand through my hair. "I'm sorry I couldn't be who you wanted me to be, but you've never been who I needed you to be, either. Maybe things were always destined to end this way. Maybe we were never meant to be a happy family." I sigh. "But I know you'll do what you have to do. If there's one thing you've taught me, it's that. So this is what I have to do."

With that, I get up and walk out of the house, maybe for the last time. Ever.

I used to think the worst thing in the world would be for my parents to know I'm gay. Now I know the worst thing in the world is to hide who I am.

I smile when I see Connor leaning against my car. I walk toward him and take him in my arms.

"How was it?" he asks, pressing a soft kiss to my lips.

I shrug. "Pretty much how I expected."

"Are you okay?"

I squeeze him tighter. "I'm better than okay."

He pulls back to look at me.

"Seriously," I say. "I have you, and that's all I need."

He kisses me again.

"Come on," he says when we break apart, "we've got one more stop to make today."

CHAPTER 37

"Your doctor?" I ask as we pull up, Connor behind the wheel. "Are you okay?" My hands start roaming all over him, trying to make sure he's okay.

He laughs. "I'm fine; it's just a checkup. Hopefully, my *last* checkup."

My eyes snap to his. "Really?"

He shrugs. "I mean, I don't know what's going on inside me, but I feel good and my incisions have healed, so I'm hopeful."

I grab the back of his neck and pull it so I can rest my forehead on his. "God, baby…."

He nods. "I know."

"I hate that I put you through all that, that you were hurting, that you were seriously injured and had an organ removed because of me."

"Hey." He cups my cheeks and holds my head so that I have no choice but to look at him. "What happened was *not* your fault. I've said it a million times, and nothing has changed since then. *I* was driving. *I* was the one who chose to drive at that speed and on the wrong side of the road. It was *all* me."

I give him a look that he gives me right back.

"I'm not backing down on this," he says.

I throw my hands up. "Fine."

He laughs and kisses me. "Good. Now get your fine ass out of the car and come hold my hand."

I raise an eyebrow.

"What? Doctors are scary, and I need my big, bad boyfriend to protect me."

Well, when he puts it that way….

"So," I say when we get back to the car.

"So," he echoes.

"A clean bill of health…."

He smiles. "I know. It feels good."

"Just good?" I ask, running my hand up and down over his thigh, close but not close enough to the dick I'm desperate to have.

He leans his head back against the headrest, eyes closed, and groans.

I lean over, taking his earlobe in between my teeth. "I believe you owe me a day in bed, babe."

Faster than I can blink, he has his seat belt on and is cranking the ignition.

The tires screech as he pulls out of the parking garage.

I chuckle. "In a hurry?"

He grabs my hand and puts it on his now hard dick.

"Okay, hurry, but not too much, please. You've just

healed from one horrific car crash; we really don't need to get into another straight after."

He laughs but does put his foot down as far as the Chicago traffic will allow.

He pulls into the garage, slipping into one of my parking spots. He turns off the car, and for a moment, we just sit, listening to the car tick as it cools.

"So," I say.

"So," he echoes again. He turns to look at me, his eyes soft. "We're free, baby."

I lean back in my seat and blow out a breath. "Yeah, I guess we are."

"Are you… you know… happy?"

I sit for a while. "I don't know if happy is the right word. I mean, I am, of course I am, but I think it's more than that. Relieved maybe? Maybe fulfilled or even complete, but yeah, whatever it is, I'm glad that it's over and done and I don't have anything to worry about. Ever again. At least when it comes to my parents."

"How do you feel about them?" he asks.

I shrug. "I don't know. I guess the easiest answer would be that I'm disappointed in them, but I always knew this was going to be their reaction and their choice, so I guess I've just had every thought about how they'd react confirmed, so I'm… comforted by that fact?" It comes out sounding like a question, but Connor gets it, regardless. He always gets it.

He nods. "It's sort of the same as when my parents died. On one hand, I didn't want them to go, but on the other, I knew once they did, they wouldn't be in pain anymore. On one hand, you didn't want to be proved right because then it means your parents are exactly as horrible as they claim to be. On the other, you know if that's the case, you'll have no problems cutting them out of your life."

I lean over and kiss him. "Our life," I say when we break apart.

"Huh?" he asks.

"You said I'd have no problem cutting them out of *my* life, but it's not just mine anymore, it's *ours*."

He smiles and rests his forehead on mine. "In that case, what do you think about starting *our* life?"

We look at each other for a millisecond before reaching for the doors.

The moment the elevator doors open, I rush him in and slam him against the wall, blindly keying in my code to get the metal box moving while attacking his neck, his lips.

Eventually it starts moving, and I can put my left hand to better use.

I unzip his fly, grabbing the boner that's fast running out of room.

He hisses through his teeth.

"This is mine, got it?" I ask.

He nods.

"Good."

The elevator dings and opens, dumping us in my, now our, living room.

"Bedroom," I murmur against his lips.

He nods, and we make our way there, clothes coming off, our lips never parting.

We make it to the room, only bumping into three walls and tripping over one rug.

I push him away from me slightly and slide down his boxers.

There's a gleam in his eye as he walks backward toward the bed.

"You think you're being coy," I tell him, "but I'm onto you."

He laughs. "Yeah?"

I nod. "Yeah, so get your ass on the bed like the good boy you are."

He does as he's told, lying face up in the middle of the bed, lazily stroking his impressive erection.

"I know you said *you* wanted to keep *me* in bed all day," I say as I crawl over him, "but this is an equal partnership, babe, and I'm taking what's mine."

"You are, are you?" He raises an eyebrow.

I grab his bottom lip with my teeth and give it a tug. "Yes, I am."

He stretches out underneath me. "Then do your worst."

I drop my body onto his, my own lighting up with the contact, our dicks rubbing deliciously against each other.

"Mmm," he moans, his hands coming round and grabbing my ass, pulling me closer.

I grab them and pull them above his head, our fingers interlacing.

"Uh-uh," I scold. "This is my show. You'll get your turn later."

His eyes flash.

"But in the meantime—" I drop a kiss on his lips. "—it's my turn to play."

I transfer his hands into one of mine, the other grabbing his dick.

"Ugh," he groans, throwing his head back, exposing his throat.

I take the opportunity presented to me, scrapping my teeth along the column.

"Oh, fuck, Cav."

I pull back. "Say that again."

He looks at me. "Oh, fuck?"

I shake my head. "The last bit."

His stare turns heated. "Babe, do you want me to say your name?"

I growl in response. He so rarely uses it, it's always babe or baby, and while the endearment gets me, it's something else entirely to hear my name come out of his mouth. He looks me in the eye. "Cavanaugh James McLaughlin, I love you with all my being, but can you quit playing and fuck me already? I'm dying here."

I chuckle but relent. "Well, when you put it that way…." I reach over to the nightstand, pulling out the new box of condoms I bought when I moved in and the bottle of lube.

"A whole box?" he asks.

I nod. "And when we've gone through that box, there's more in the bathroom."

His eyes flash.

"Sound good to you?" I ask.

"Yeah, t-that sounds fine."

I chuckle and lean down to kiss him. "Good."

I hitch his leg higher on my hip, sliding my hand down his thigh, and squeeze his ass.

I groan. "Damn, Con, this ass of yours, baby…."

He looks up at me. "You know how you asked me to say your name before?" he asks.

"Yeah?"

He stretches up to kiss me. "I *totally* get it now."

"Yeah? You like it?"

He shakes his head. "No, I *love* it."

I kiss him. "I love you."

He struggles against my hand, still holding him down. I relent and release one. He cups my cheek.

"And I love you."

"You ready for this?" I ask, grabbing the bottle of lube.

He nods. "Do your worst, babe."

I squirt some of the liquid on my finger, tracing his rim and making him squirm.

"Cav," he whines.

I chuckle. "Saying my name isn't going to get your way every time," I tell him.

He groans. "You're such a bastard."

I kiss him for no other reason than I can and want to. "I am, but you love it."

He rolls his eyes and pushes his ass against my hand.

I spank him, the crack against his flesh such a satisfying sound my cock jerks, and I know precum is leaking out of me. It's not helped by Connor's moan.

"You like that?" I ask.

He nods. "Yeah," he breathes.

I do it again, and he moans louder.

I chuckle. "Underneath that good boy, there's a definite bad boy, isn't there?"

I thrust against him, our dicks rubbing against each other, sending a rush of pleasure like I've never known through me.

"You're such a tease," he says, eyes and mouth tight.

I lean down, grabbing his earlobe in my teeth. "I'm all bad boy, baby."

I spank him one more time before plunging my finger in his ass.

"Jesus Christ!" he yells, jacking up off the bed, cum spurting between our slicked bodies.

"Shit," he pants, slumping back against the mattress.

"Mmm," I moan as I continue to work my finger in and out of him. "That was a good one."

He scrubs his hand over his face. "That was embarrassing as fuck. I thought I had more control than that." He looks down at the mess he made between our bodies.

I swipe at a drop of the pearly liquid and stick my finger in my mouth, his salty taste flooding my mouth. "It makes me wild knowing I can do that to you, that you have that reaction to me."

"Yeah?"

I withdraw my finger from his ass, grab some more lube, and go back with a second. He moans when I breach him. I thrust into him as if it were my cock inside him, not my fingers.

"Yeah," I pant. "I want everything from you, your pain."

I spank him again, and his dick jerks to attention again. "Your pleasure." I stroke his prostate. "I want that and everything in between."

"Fuck, Cav...." His hands come around me, nails digging into my back.

"Can you give that to me?" I ask.

He opens his eyes. "Can you give that to *me*?" he counters.

I lean down and kiss him. "That and *so* much more."

He cups my cheek again, and I nuzzle into the touch. "Right back atcha."

I withdraw my hand and add some more lube before returning with three fingers.

"Nothing can break us," I tell him. "No one else can get in here. It's just you and me against the world, got it?"

"There's nothing I want more," he tells me, eyes bright, staring straight into my soul.

"Fuck this," I say, withdrawing my hand. I grab the box of condoms, ripping it open and snatching at one of the foil squares. I rip open the second one in the strip in my haste, but I don't care. They'll all get used, anyway. I put it on with shaking hands.

"Hey," Connor says, stopping me. "Breathe. It's okay, we have all the time in the world."

I do as he says.

"That's better," he coos. "Now, come here."

He pulls me down, legs wrapping around my hips, ankles locking behind me, his arms going around my chest, not letting me go.

"Hi," he says.

"Uh, hi," I reply.

He chuckles, and the sound goes straight to my heart. Never did I ever think I'd be here. *We'd* be here. But I am. We are. When I first saw Connor's profile on that app, I thought he'd be perfect for a hookup. Then we started talking, and I knew, if I let it, I could be in trouble.

Then when I saw him the first day at school, I thought my world was ending. To an extent, it was. My old world ended. Against Connor, it never stood a chance.

He tore my world down. But together we've built it back up. Stronger, truer.

"There he is," Connor says, smiling.

"Who?"

"The guy I always knew you could be."

I roll my eyes.

He grabs my chin. "No. Don't do that. Don't downplay what's happening here, what has already happened. You're here. We're here." He stops and swallows. "When my parents were sick and dying, so much of my life was about Jase. Looking after him, making sure he had everything he needed. I put my wants and needs aside to look after him. Then I came across your profile and I thought 'wouldn't it be nice to have something, some*one* just for myself?' We did it the hard way." He reaches down and gives me a jerk. "The *very* hard way, but we're here, Cav. We fucking made it."

I lean down and kiss him.

"Yeah, we fucking did," I say as I push inside him.

"Oh God, you're fucking huge," he says, throwing his head back.

"You'll get used to me," I reply.

He looks back at me. "Yeah, I guess I will."

We move together, our bodies in harmony, sweat pouring off us.

"You feel so good, Con," I tell him. "I never want to leave."

"That could… pose some… p-problems," he pants.

"I'm willing to work them out," I say, never pausing my thrusting.

He chuckles. "I bet you arrrrrrrrrrrrrrrrrrrrrrrrrrrrrrrrrrre," he replies as I thrust deep and hard. "Yeah, just there, baby."

I do it again and again until he's writhing underneath me, my own movements becoming more frenzied the longer we continue.

"Cav, I'm going to come," he tells me.

"So come," I say into his ear. "I'll be with you all the way."

I've barely finished speaking when his climax erupts between us.

"Fuuuuuuuuuuuuuuuuuuck," I moan as I empty myself into the condom.

I collapse onto his sweaty chest, his arms holding me tight.

"We're catching our breath for a minute," he says. "And then we're going through all those boxes you have."

CHAPTER 38

We did go through the box in the bedroom, as well as most of the one in the bathroom, and by the end, both of us were exhausted. Well-fucked and sated, but exhausted.

My alarm goes off, and Connor buries his head in my neck, groaning.

"Don't say it."

I chuckle. "We have to get up."

He groans again. "I can't walk."

I jerk up. "What? Are you hurt? Was I too rough? Do you need a doctor?"

He puts a hand to my chest and pushes me back down. "I'm fine, but my boyfriend fucked me six ways to Sunday yesterday, and I'm still coming down from the orgasmic high he sent me on."

"Oh." I relax against the bed while Connor snuggles into my side. I kiss the top of his head. "Good morning," I whisper.

"Don't be sweet when you're going to make me get out of this bed," he says.

"We're going to have to at some stage."

"So? Doesn't mean it has to be *now*." He throws his leg over mine.

I smack his ass.

"That's not gonna help your cause," he tells me, his morning wood jerking against my thigh.

I roll over so I'm on top of him. "I didn't realize you were such a bad boy in bed," I say as I push his hair off his forehead.

He shrugs. "What can I say? You bring it out in me."

I lean down and kiss him. "And I'm *so* glad I do."

His chuckle turns to a groan as I roll my hips against him.

"Now that's *really* not helping."

"Maybe you've convinced me to be bad."

His hands roam down to my ass. "You've always been the bad boy."

I nip his ear. "Yes, I am." I reach for the lube.

"So what was with the good boy act just then?" he asks.

I shrug. "I was trying it out."

"And?"

I snap open the cap and squirt some on my finger. "What do you think?"

I'm in my happy place inside Connor when his phone rings.

"Ignore it," I beg as I thrust.

He looks at the screen. "It's Jase; it could be important."

I pull out and encourage him onto all fours. "Give me two minutes," I say, slapping his ass and grabbing his boner.

Fifteen minutes later—we both have reputations to protect—he calls Jase back as I clean up.

I'm glad I'm at a good place with Jase. I know he's always going to worry about Connor, just as Connor is always going to worry about him, but neither of them have anything to worry about. I meant it when I said I would take care of Connor for the rest of my life. And I will. And Jase will find his way in the world. He's a great kid and I will never fault anyone for looking out for Connor, even if that means going against me. Nah, the kid's all right.

Plus, Connor is a permanent fixture in my life, so that means Jase will be as well.

"Jase wants to see us," Connor says after he ends the call.

I nod. "Okay."

"He heard about the article and wanted to check in on us."

"*Both* of us?" I ask.

He nods, a smile on his face. "Yeah, both of us. Is that okay?"

I swallow the lump in my throat. "Ah, yeah, that's um, fine."

He comes up to me and cups my face in his hands. "Are you okay?"

I nod.

"Are you sure? A lot went on yesterday."

"Yeah, I'm fine."

"And Thomas?" he asks.

I blow out a breath. "Thomas will get his. He's done all the damage he can and now we can forget about him."

"You don't want revenge?"

"Of course I do, but I think I've more than proved that sometimes my actions do more harm than good."

"Really?" he asks, arching an eyebrow.

I chuckle. "Yes, Connor, really."

His eyes flare when I say his name, something I find myself doing more and more just so I can get that reaction.

He cocks his head to the side, and I sigh. "Look, I know this isn't how you'd expect me to react, but I'm… trying to be better. For you. Because of you. Before we met, I was…. Well, I was an asshole. I know that. I actively encouraged that reputation and lived up to it. I had to if I wanted to hide, you know, things."

His eyes soften, and he nods.

"But now, with you, I don't have to hide. I don't *want* to hide. To be honest, it's a relief. Being an asshole, not letting anything slip by, even something small, was exhausting. I won't say I hated it, 'cause I didn't—well not *all* the time anyway, and it was nice having everyone jump at my every command, but…."

"But every now and then you wanted some pushback, someone to challenge you," he finishes for me.

"Does that make me weird?" I ask.

He shakes his head. "I think that makes you

redeemable. You realized you had too much power and you wanted someone to keep you in check."

I hug him to me. "You make me sound a lot more gallant than it was. Maybe I just get off on people being mean to me."

He chuckles and bites my shoulder. "For your dick's sake, the only person you're allowed to get off on being mean to you better be me."

I lift his head. "No one hurts me as bad as you do, babe."

He stretches to kiss me. "Good. Now I suppose we should finally get ready and go see my brother."

I kiss him one last time. "Good thing I set the alarm half an hour early, isn't it?" I take off toward the bathroom while he growls and chases me.

He might be helping me to be good, but there will always be a bit of bad.

CHAPTER 39

We managed to get ready with minimal disruptions before swinging by to pick Jase up. Connor's relationship with Amy is… iffy at best. While she accepted the accident wasn't Connor's fault, I think it exposed a deeper mistrust that can't really be fixed. And while he spends most, well, basically *all* of his nights at the penthouse, he still technically lives with his brother and sister.

"Do you need to grab anything while we're here?" I ask as we pull up, me behind the wheel today.

He shakes his head. "Not really. Besides, if I need anything, I'll just use yours."

I chuckle. "Guess that's one advantage to having a boyfriend."

He runs his hand over my thigh as he leans toward me. "One of *many*," he purrs before his lips find mine.

We're interrupted by Jase opening the car door. "Ah, do you guys want me to come back in a few minutes?"

We finish the kiss before I try to rearrange my now tight pants.

"Nah, man, you're good," I tell him. "Get in."

"So you guys are okay, then?" he asks, getting in and shutting the door.

I nod. "Yeah, we're fine."

"Good. I was worried the article would cause problems."

"I mean, it caused problems, but not between the two of us." If I have my way, there will never be any problems between Connor and me.

"Oh no, not that, I know you two are solid. I meant in a bigger sense."

"Oh, um, there were some, but we handled them."

"Good," he says.

I look to Connor. "So, is that it?" I ask.

Jase nods. "Pretty much."

"Okaaaaaaaaaaaaaaaay," I reply.

Jase looks to Connor. "What? I can't be concerned about my brother's boyfriend and no doubt future brother-in-law?"

My throat is tight. Connor grabs my hand and squeezes.

"That's really sweet, Jase. Thank you."

He shrugs. "I figure I've given you two my own fair amount of shit, I should probably start paying it back."

I shake my head. "Y-You don't have to pay anything back," I tell him.

He looks to me. "Yes, I do. You're good for Connor. You protect him. You love him. You make him happy.

That's all I've ever wanted for him and I'm glad he's found someone who can do that."

I can't stop the tear that rolls down my cheek. "T-Thank you," I manage to croak out.

He nods. "So, what are we going to do about Thomas?" he asks.

"What do you mean, *we*?" Connor asks, his big brother voice more than on.

"He was the one who went to the paper, right? Surely you guys won't let that slide."

I look to Connor and squeeze his hand. "We don't know where he is," I tell Jase. "He sent me a photo of him on a beach somewhere, but aside from that…."

"So hire a PI, track that loser down."

I shrug. "I could do that. I could track him down and have him charged with distribution of child pornography and probably a few other things, but I know Thomas would keep coming at me. He'd keep coming, and keep coming, and keep coming, and where does it end?" I blow out a breath. "After all the things I've done over the past two years, I'm tired. I'm tired of fighting, of hiding, of worrying about someone finding out my secret, of someone spilling it to the senator or the papers. Is it so bad if I just want to leave it and live my life?"

Connor and I talked about this last night in between bouts of earth-shattering sex. He gets where I'm coming from, and he's more than happy to let me take the lead on this one.

Jase tilts his head. "Well, when you put it that way…."

I chuckle. "I appreciate you taking up for me, more than you know, but I think that's where I'm at, where *we're* at right now. We just want to go about our lives and be happy."

Jase nods. "Then that's what we'll do."

"And we're okay, right?" I ask him. "You're not pissed at me, you're not pissed at Connor, we're all happy families?"

"We are. I see how much you love my brother and that's enough for me."

"I do," I tell him. "With my whole heart, body, and soul."

He scrunches his nose. "I think I can live without knowing how much loving your bodies do."

My cheeks heat, but we chuckle.

"Oh, my god! Cavanaugh McLaughlin, are you *blushing*?" Connor asks.

"What? No!"

"You are! Oh my God! That's *so* cute! You're embarrassed about my brother knowing about our sex life!"

"Okay, I think that's enough," I say, turning to face the front again.

"Seriously? You can blow me in a janitor's closet at school, but you don't want Jase to know we have earth-shattering sex?"

I try to cover his mouth as Jase says, "You guys hooked up in a *janitor's closet*? That's *so* gross."

I look back at him. "What can I say? Your brother's hot."

He pretends to gag.

We chuckle.

. . .

"Well, well, well," Chloe says as we all get out of the car. "If it isn't the merry fucking *Brady Bunch*."

"Morning to you too, gorgeous," Connor says, kissing her cheek.

"I saw the article," she says to me.

I shrug. "You and half of Chicago, plus the political half of DC."

"You okay?" Chloe asks.

I shrug. "They took the article down. It's all good."

She nods. "And your parents?"

"Done with me for good." Connor takes my hand and kisses the back of it.

"And that's…?"

"A good thing," I finish for her. "Now I'm free to live my life how I want, with whom I want."

"All right, then."

"How are you?" Connor asks, changing the subject. "How's Sienna?"

She scoffs as we walk into the building. "That cock whore? I saw her with Hunter Harris all over my socials on the weekend."

"I hear he's touted as a future president," I say.

Chloe rolls her eyes. "Whatever. Everyone knows men only go into politics for a power trip 'cause they have tiny dicks."

"Which rules us out," I say, slinging an arm around Connor's neck and pulling him close.

"You say the sweetest things, babe," he says before kissing me.

"Get a room," Chloe says, rolling her eyes. "C'mon,

Jase." She threads an arm through his and continues walking down the hall, the crowd quickly swallowing them up.

"You okay?" Connor asks.

"Huh? Oh, yeah, I'm good." I hug him tighter to me.

We get a few looks as we walk down the hall, but no one says anything. Whether that's because they're scared to or they genuinely have nothing to say, I don't really care.

I used to think that people finding out who I am would be the worst thing in the world. And yeah, at first it was terrifying, but you know what? People can surprise you. That's never so apparent as with the guy, my boyfriend, my *heart*, who's walking next to me.

I never thought I'd find someone who made me want to risk it all. I thought I was destined to be in the closet my entire life, only coming out every now and then, becoming one of those creepy guys who liked to live it up when the wife wasn't watching. It wasn't a reality I relished, but it was one I accepted.

Until Connor.

He changed my life. He *saved* my life.

Who knows how long I would've survived having to hide, to always cover my tracks, to not be who I really am.

It hasn't been easy, but what relationship is? But I think we're better because of our struggles. We're *stronger* because of them. I know I can count on him. I hope he knows he can count on me. Because he can. I may not be an angel, but for him? This bad boy might just turn good.

Ten years later.
Cancun, Mexico.

"**P**apa! Papa!" our son, Rowan, calls as he runs along the beach. "Look what Dad, Camille, and I found!"

I lean back in my seat and look out over the sand.

Connor and I moved down here seven years ago. We tried the whole college thing, but it wasn't really for us. The work wasn't difficult, but the people…. Everyone was so excited to begin their "adult" lives. Adult, ha! College life isn't adult life, it's like almost-adult life, and we'd already lived enough to know school wasn't for us.

By high school graduation, Connor and I were living together in all but name, paying our own bills, making sure the penthouse, our cars, everything, were up to scratch. Sure, we each had strong financial backing, but compared to what those college students thought life was? We couldn't take it.

So we packed up and drove. Then we kept on driving and ended up here.

We have our own little bar right here on the beach, as well as a restaurant in town. Chloe's wife, an up-and-coming chef from San Francisco, helped us set it up.

A year after we moved, we felt something, no, some*one* was missing.

So we adopted Rowan, just like Connor said he wanted.

Chloe offered us an egg and use of her uterus for nine months, but that's not what we wanted. We have offered her use of our sperm should she and Mel want it, though.

We welcomed Rowan five years ago, Camille, three.

Rowan races up the steps to where I'm sitting, and I drag him on my lap, a generous coating of sand coming with him.

I kiss his sandy head. "What did you find, buddy?"

Being a dad… it's like nothing on this earth. When we got the notice that we had been approved, then when we saw Rowan for the first time…. Nothing could ever top that moment. It does share equal billing with Camille, though.

And so our kids have two dads, or a dad and a papa, and more love than they can handle at times. But it's amazing. I never thought I could love anyone more than I love Connor. Then our kids came along and bam! I'd give anything, absolutely anything, for my kids.

Rowan taps my cheek. "Papa, are you listening?" he asks.

I kiss his head again. "Of course. Tell me, what did you find?"

"We found treasure," he breathes, his brown eyes wide and bright.

"Treasure, huh?"

He nods. "Yup. I found lots, but I gave some to Cammie 'cause she's not as good at finding as I am."

I give him a squeeze. "You're such a good big brother. Thank you for that."

He puffs up his little chest. "It's no big deal. She's my sister, so I gotta protect her and love her and be nice to her."

I chuckle. "That's right."

Connor and Camille come up the steps.

"I hear you had a very bountiful day today," I say, scooping my daughter up and squeezing her on my lap next to her brother, while Connor flops into a chair next to me.

Cammie nods and holds up two shells.

"Wow! Look at those!" I gush.

"Wowo finded them for me," she says.

"He's a good big brother, isn't he?" I ask.

She nods, her blonde curls flying everywhere.

"All right, you two, dinner will be ready soon, so let's get you all cleaned up, all right?"

"Thanks, babe," Connor says as I walk past, a kid on each hip.

I wink and blow a kiss at him.

L ater that night we're lying in bed, catching our breath after one hell of a bout of lovemaking. Yes, I'm that gone. No, I don't give a fuck.

I snort.

"What?" Connor asks, turning his head to face me.

"I just realized I referred to this as 'lovemaking' in my head."

He chuckles. "That's as good a term as any."

I roll to face him. "Did you honestly think ten years ago, we'd be calling sex lovemaking?" I ask.

He shakes his head. "No, but back then, all I was interested in was getting your dick in my mouth. Or mine in yours. I wasn't picky."

I snort again. "You *still* want that."

He shrugs and runs a hand over my chest. "My husband is hot, what can I say?"

Did I forget to mention we got married the day after our high school graduation? Chloe got ordained online and performed the ceremony.

I moan as his hand slides lower, lower, lower, before finally taking hold of my rapidly hardening dick.

"Fuck, I love how you react to me, Cav, baby. Always have, always will."

I roll on top of him, pinning his free hand above his head.

"I guess it's a good thing you push all my buttons then, huh?"

"Oh, I'll push *all* your buttons, baby."

I chuckle and lean down to kiss him.

Instead, he grabs my bottom lip between his teeth and pulls.

I growl.

"Be bad for me, babe," he urges. "Show me just how bad you can be."

So I do, because if there's one thing I know, you can never keep a bad boy down for long.

THE END

USEFUL LINKS

If you have been affected by any of the issues discussed in this book, please know there are various resources available to you to help get you through your tough time. These are only a very small selection. Please reach out if you, or someone you love needs help. **You are wanted, you are valued, you have a place here.**

Australia.
Lifeline: 13 11 44
QLife: 1800 184 527

Canada.
Canada Suicide Prevention Service: 1 833 456 4566
LGBT Youth Crisis Line: 1800 268 9688

The UK.
Assistline: 0800 689 5652
Mind: 0300 123 3393

<u>The United States.</u>
National Suicide Prevention Lifeline: 1800 273 8255
The Trevor Project: 1 866 488 7386

Two is Better Than One – Boys like Girls featuring Taylor Swift.
Welcome to my Life – Simple Plan.
Summer Paradise – Simple Plan featuring K'naan.
Addicted – Simple Plan.
I'd Do Anything – Simple Plan.
Perfect – Simple Plan.
Monsters – All Time Low.
Something's Gotta Give – All Time Low.
Dirty Laundry – All Time Low.
Numb – Linkin Park.
What I've Done – Linkin Park.
Heavy – Linkin Park featuring Kiiara.
Dirty Little Secret – All American Rejects.
Sweat – All American Rejects.
Boulevard of Broken Dreams – Green Day.
Angel with a Shotgun – The Cab.
Intoxicated – The Cab.
Endlessly – The Cab.

Bad – The Cab.
Secrets – OneRepublic.
Run – OneRepublic.
Rescue Me – OneRepublic.
Hot Mess – Cobra Starship.
Good Girls go Bad – Cobra Starship featuring Leighton Meester.
Middle Finger – Cobra Starship featuring Mac Miller.
Teenagers – My Chemical Romance.
This Ain't a Scene, It's an Arms Race – Fall Out Boy.
Irresistible – Fall Out Boy.
Caution – The Killers.
All These Things That I've Done – The Killers.
The Only Exception – Paramore.
Still into You – Paramore.
Under Pressure – Queen.
Born this Way – Lady Gaga.
Gravity – Papa Roach.
Only One – Yellowcard.
Into The Unknown – Panic! At the Disco.

ACKNOWLEDGMENTS

So these books were a long time coming, huh? I'm *so* sorry for the break! I had a super tight deadline for *Royal Blue* and pushed myself to the limit for that book. I hope it shows; I love that book something fierce! Afterwards, I rolled straight into *Regal Purple*. I had an editing date, and was looking at hitting that fairly comfortably when I sat down to revise and couldn't stand to read what was on the page in front of me.

That had never happened to me before, and to be honest, it scared me a little bit too. Was I broken? Was I destined to hate everything I ever wrote for the rest of time? I spoke to some friends and we all agreed that I burnt myself out on *Royal Blue*. That's not a bad thing; it's just what happened. It happens.

So I took some time. And then I took some more time. And then Covid happened and we were all thrown into another world. I work in retail so it was a whirlwind for me for sure. Writing was the last thing on my mind. Making sure people had toilet paper, flour, sugar, hand sanitiser; all that good stuff was what occupied my thoughts.

And then things got better. Restrictions eased. In Australia we were so incredibly lucky. We continue to be lucky. I pray that it stays like that.

But I had more time on my hands, and less stress. I could read again. And reading for me always gets my mind wondering. I'd had the idea for this duet for a while now. I think, in a weird twist of fate, I had always kind of slated these books for release around now anyway. I just had planned for there to be more in between. Oh well. They'll come.

Writing these books took me a lot longer than they normally would, but what is normal now anyway? But I got there. I was rusty as hell, and I know my editor would agree with me! It took a while for me to get back into the swing of things, but here we are! I hope you love my boys!

First and foremost I want to thank my parents, especially my Mum for recognising my stress levels were off the chart, and reminding me to take a breath.

I also want to thank for her for warning my Dad about my stress levels and telling him not to push me. I want to thank him for listening to her!

I also want to thank my editor, Liv. There is no one else I trust to shape my words. You know what I mean, even when I'm not very clear about what it is I'm getting at, and know exactly when to push me. Thank you for helping me grow.

I also want to thank everyone else at Hot Tree Editing

who had a hand in these books. Your help and expertise is most greatly appreciated.

Next up are my beautiful book friends; Ang, Gen, Mary, and Trysh. You four keep me grounded, you listen to me vent, you tell me what's real and I appreciate you all so much.

I want to thank Dez at Pretty In Ink Creations for her amazing covers, and formatting prowess.

I also to thank Eric McKinney and Mark S for the photo on the cover of this book in particular. As soon as I saw Mark, I knew I had to have him on one of my covers. There is no one else who could've been my Cav.

I want to thank Shauna at Wildfire Marketing for helping get the word out about these books, and every single blogger, bookstagrammer, and booktoker who signed up.

Finally, I want to thank you, the reader who has made it this far! Thank you so much for giving my boys a chance. I do hope you'll leave a review. Your words mean just as much as mine do!

And a final message to anyone who has been affected by the themes discussed in this book. You are wanted, you are loved, you have a place here. *Please* seek help if you need it. It might not feel like it today, but you do make our world a better place.

ABOUT MEGAN

Megan Lowe is a lost journalism graduate who after many painful years searching for a job in that field, decided if she couldn't write news stories, she would start listening to the characters whispering stories to her and decided to write them down.

She writes primarily Mature YA/New Adult/Contemporary Romance stories with a difference.

She is based on the Gold Coast but her heart belongs to New York City.

When she's not writing she's either curled up with a good book, travelling or screaming at the TV willing her sporting teams to pull out the win.

STALKER LINKS!

Website:
www.meganloweauthor.wixsite.com/withadifference

Facebook:
www.facebook.com/MeganLoweAuthor

Amazon:
www.amazon.com/author/meganlowe

Bookbub:
www.bookbub.com/authors/megan-lowe

Goodreads:
www.goodreads.com/meganlowereads

Instagram:
www.instagram.com/meganloweauthor

Twitter:
www.twitter.com/meganloweauthor

meganloweauthor@outlook.com

Sign up to my newsletter:

https://t.co/M31GCdcYtL

Rocking Racers Series

Breaking the Cycle

No Place to Hide

Breaking Away

Breaking Down

All I Want

Breaking Free

Breaking Out

Breaking Ground

Read today here: books2read.com/rl/rocking-racers

Sovereigns of Savannah

Royal Blue

The Good Boy/Bad Boy duet

Good Boy

Bad Boy